Contents

collection and supporting me during its compilation, and to those friends, particularly Brian Turner, who gave advice when I asked for it.

As its sub-title suggests, this book is about writing as well as fishing. My hope is that the two come together well here.

Owen Marshall

Note: Fishers use a mixture of imperial and metric measurements and this collection follows that inconsistency.

They Call Me Jonah

~

ROGER HALL

They call me Jonah.

I've been fishing for years. It's just that the fish don't know this. Just as certain New Zealand batsmen often 'fail to trouble the scorers', so I fail to trouble the fish. A garden gnome dangling his line into a goldfish pond has a better strike rate than me.

Worse. It's not just that *I* don't get fish, very often if I'm in a group *no one* gets fish.

It all goes back a long way. My parents used to take me for typical British sea-side holidays at places like Eastbourne and Worthing. Many shops along the front sold shrimp nets. They were pleasing to the eye, nice triangular neat nets on top of poles. Each summer, kids and adults in their thousands bought them. I never, ever, saw anyone catch a shrimp.

One year I bought a line. Many yards of line, plus sinker and several hooks were attached to a wooden square. You unwound it, lowering it into the water.

Eagerly I set off to the pier to try it out for the first time.

'Don't drop it,' warned my father in one of those typical and useless bits of parental advice.

I dropped it. The yards of line, hooks and sinker went straight to the bottom.

So though I failed to catch a fish during my childhood, at least I never blighted anyone else's chances. That didn't happen until 30 years or so later when my brother-in-law took me to Napier's West Shore to launch his Kon-tiki with me.

There was the perfect wind for it. Ian baited the many hooks and off it went, a grand sight, on and on out to its full length. Then the line snapped, but of course the Kon-tiki kept going and for all I know it is sailing away from shore to this very day.

At Whakatane a friend had gone out in a boat the previous week and caught so many fish that her dinghy was in danger of capsizing. So enthusiastic was Paula for her husband and me to share the experience that she booked us on a fishing trip that would be covering the same fishing spots where she'd made the great catch. There were at least a dozen people on board, all with their lines out, and the skipper took us to Paula's place and to many other reliable spots as well. No one on board caught a fish.

At Stewart Island it is impossible not to catch blue cod. Everybody knows that. The crew knows that on the homeward leg of the cruise its job is to gut and fillet the passengers' catch, and once back on shore to freeze them ready to be taken home. It's a tourist industry. But not when I'm on board. We set off, the skipper found the spot, cut the engines and peered at the sonar. 'They're there!' he exclaimed. Fifteen lines were lowered into the water. Twenty minutes later, no one on board had got a bite, so the skipper moved to another sure-fire area. He peered at his sonar again. 'They're there!' This pattern was repeated twice more before he headed for home. And the end of the trip, no one troubled the freezer. It should have gone into the Guinness Book of Negative Records.

Okay. I admit it. I *have* caught blue cod in the Sounds. My other brother-in-law took me out and I dangled my line overboard and yes, this time, there were frequent tugs and we did haul them up and within an hour were eating them for lunch. Fish has never tasted better.

But listen, none of this is real fishing. Real fishing is fly fishing and everyone knows it.

I had been in Dunedin for a few years and it slowly dawned on me that I was living in one of the great fly fishing areas in the world. Furthermore you didn't have to be rich or have blue blood in your veins to have access to a river as you did in many parts of the world. I realised I was crazy not to try it. But first I tried for salmon. Smolt had been released into Otago Harbour to increase the numbers of other salmon bred in the headwaters of the Waitaki and other rivers. Each year they started returning, fully grown, into the harbour when you could stand on the wharf and fish for them there, or drive miles to Harington Point and fish for them there. I did both. Casting out, winding in, hour after hour. I failed to trouble the scorers.

So fly fishing it was to be. I made my first mistake: I signed up for lessons. The lessons were good, but really it is much better to go out and try something a few times and then you know what it is you need to know.

The lessons were given at Logan Park High School in the evenings by Mike Weddell who had twice been world champion fly caster, competing in Scotland to win. Gold medal stuff but hardly anyone in the country knew about it. I guess TVNZ's European correspondent was too busy reporting on rail or ferry boat disasters to bother about such triumphs.

There were a few middle-aged blokes like me taking the class, but most were recent retirees who thought they'd take up a new hobby now they had the time. Mike Weddell told them: 'You've left it too late', which wasn't very tactful of him but his dramatic way of pointing out that it takes 15 years to make a fly fisherman.

In class I showed such promise. Everything Mike said made sense. 'Find out what the fish are feeding on and tie on the appropriate fly.' Well of *course*! I was the only one who knew what the most expensive part of fishing was (petrol). At Logan Park when we practised casting on the grass one summer's evening I was great. Could land the fly on a specific daisy. Then the class headed south to the Mataura (regardless of expense) for its first practical session. Lesson one, spot the fish. Well there weren't any. You looked at the river and there were no fish in it, it was as simple as that. But Mike ran up and down the river bank shouting, 'There's one!' and then from somewhere else, 'There's one!' And sure enough there *was* one. And though it often wasn't easy, you began to get the knack of knowing where to look and experience that tiny kick of the heart when you saw one.

Of course, when you saw a fish you had to choose a fly. Can there ever be such an enticing catalogue of names as there is for flies? The nymphs: Hare's Ear, Stonefly, Pheasant Tail. Dry flies: Cochybondhu, Adam's, Royal Wulff, Black Gnat, Twilight Beauty, Green Beetle, Tup's Indispensible, Love's Lure, Greenwell's Glory. There are hundreds more but surely none can surpass for appropriateness (and my perpetual thanks to the genius who thought of it) that wonderful name for a lure: Mrs Simpson.

So seeing a fish meant tying a fly. No, no, not tying a fly, tying them is *making* the things, delicate craftsmanship and design, tiny works of art, no no, I never once contemplated that. I mean tying them *on*. Even at home, warm and dry, it was difficult enough. But on a river bank, when it was wet and windy, it was torture for the fingers. I felt the phrase, 'his fingers were all thumbs', had been coined about me.

Okay, fish spotted, now to cast. And, of course, what had been simple at Logan Park was anything but on the river bank. I cast confidently, then spent many minutes removing the fly from the bushes I failed to notice behind me.

At the end of our day on the river, no one had landed a fish (except Mike). But still, I had a new hobby.

And, as with new pastimes, a whole new world opens up to you of things to buy: clothing, gear, special little scissors, lines and leaders. I stupidly bought one of those collapsible rods advertised on the back page of the *Listener*, so that I'd always have it in the car. First time it was used, it collapsed permanently, and soon afterwards so did the mail-order firm that sold it to me. But for a time my new hobby solved the Christmas present problem for my family. The kids bought me a hat and a junior book on fishing, and Dianne bought me one of those armless fishing jackets, the ones with lots and lots of pockets (hopeless, of course; it means you search through every pocket for whatever it is you want, complete the circuit and find it back in the first pocket).

So now I had the gear and the knowledge. Time to go fishing. Preferably with people who knew what they were doing and who could help me. Mike Cooper took me to the Taieri in the evenings. It was lovely in the dusk, casting over the waters. That was all I did. Mike had better luck most nights and once, when he was with another friend, he caught a monster. It took him 20 minutes to land, and by the time he did it was dark. When Mike got it close to the shore and bent down to put his hand round its gills it wouldn't fit. Mike panicked and fell on it. Worth it, though—it weighed 9 pounds 6 ounces (damned if I'm going to put that into metrics).

Mike was one of many friends who took me fishing. Grahame Sydney patiently stood by for a time as I cast into the Clutha. Nephew Brian took me in the North Island (pooh tush, a fig for the North Island, hopeless, who'd ever bother after the South?) to the Mohaka where the only thing I caught was the crutch of my trousers on a barbed wire fence.

'No fish in *this river*,' I said as neither of us even saw one. But Brian told me some guys had once *scuba*-ed down to the bottom of a pool and counted 70. Jonah had struck again.

Another Brian, Turner, an expert, impatient with my casting style, hugged me from behind in order to hold my arms demonstrate how and why. Nowadays the *Woman's Weekly* would have a cover story: '"Not Gay" says cricket-legend brother'.

Sometimes I went by myself. It was just as easy not to catch fish alone as it was with a friend. I fished long evenings in the Clutha near Mount Pisa where for a few years we had use of a farm cottage. One Christmas I cast into the waters of the Tutaekuri, near Napier, not noticing that no one else was doing so because at that time of year the water was too warm for trout.

The best 'fishing' was at Dick Fraser's Cedar Lodge, Makarora. In return for modest help from me with a brochure, he repaid me many times over by letting me stay and treating me the same way as he did the well-heeled guests who flew in from the USA. Syd and I rolled up one evening for a couple of days' stay. Now I know Brian Turner feels passionately that one shouldn't fish in an area one can't reach by foot and there's a lot in that argument. But any principles along those lines were forgotten when Dick took Syd and me in his helicopter over the Young Range and dropped us down on the banks of the Hunter and said he'd be back at 5. On the way Dick scared us by telling us tales about helicopters: about the time Dick was almost out of fuel, lost in clouds, couldn't see anything below but had to risk everything by going straight down. About how a man was loading culled deer on to the net under the helicopter, the machine took off and later, at 1000 feet, the pilot realised that the man was dangling upside down underneath: the machine had snagged on a hole in his sock and there were only a few strands of wool between him and death. Lies, of course, all lies. The man is a fisherman after all.

Dick told me his policy for all his clients was 'catch and release'. In the event I caught anything, I told him firmly that my policy was 'catch, keep, photograph, flaunt, boast and eat'. Luckily I never had to make the decision.

That night, we dined with the guests at Dick's Lodge. How did I get onto politics and dismissing Reagan as a bumbling fool? I caught sight of a flushed, angry Republican face at the head of the table, reminded myself that this man was paying several hundred dollars a day and didn't want his holiday spoiled by some local with idiotic political opinions and *who couldn't even catch a fish*. I shut up.

The next day we were choppered up the Wilkin, the river clear, the scenery heart-stoppingly superb. Once again I failed to trouble the scorers. It didn't matter, of course: I had seen places I wouldn't otherwise have.

I *did* catch one once on the Makarora, but it was a Clayton's catch. Monty Wright, a field officer of Fish and Game Otago, gave a day's fishing lessons one summer and a group of us tyros stood in the river casting back and forth to Monty's instructions. Of course, if you didn't spot a fish, you cast to a place where a trout was likely to be. Monty demonstrated this perfectly. He grabbed my rod, cast to a place where the water broke over rocks, and within seconds had a bite. He handed the rod for me to land it. Nice, but not the real thing.

I was regaling some of these experiences at university one morning tea, and a fishing fanatic from the history department told me off. 'You don't take it seriously enough. It's no use going once every few weeks and just fishing for a bit. You need to go for several days at a time and do it properly.' He was right, of course. Brian Turner once paid me the honour of asking me to go with him and Dave Witherow on a fishing trip for several days. It was about a couple of days more than I could spare. That might have been the final apprenticeship I needed.

Well, of course, I've been holding out on you. I have caught a trout. One hot hot day Mike Cooper took me down to Gore to fish on the Mataura. It was so hot that later that night I discovered the underside of my arms agonisingly burnt from the sun reflected off the river. So hot that after a couple of hours I had to get into the water. There was no one nearby, only a group of locals 200 yards up river. I slipped out of shirt, trousers and pants and slid gently into the water. I crouched discreetly in the cold waters and experienced shrinkage.

But not discreetly enough, it seemed. It was like letting a cat into a hen house, such were the indignant squawks coming from the group upstream. I was impressed by their eyesight.

But what did I care. For that was the afternoon I caught a fish. *The* fish. By late that afternoon I was casting automatically. Bored. My mind was miles away. And then the merest tug-tug-tug. My heart stopped: this was it! I forgot everything about playing the fish. All I remembered was that the line had to be kept taut. Right, taut it would be. I walked backwards, rod held high, until the fish lay on the bank. Legal limit. Just. Mike came over. Did I want to keep it? Silly question. He knocked it on the head. I carried it home in triumph. Did I eat it? Yes. Did I photograph it? No. It was laughably small.

However, in the end I did get a fish that I photographed. The hours, the hundreds of dollars, the line cast thousands of times, eventually paid off. On my wall is a picture of me, proudly holding a large trout. But, alas, if you look closely enough, you'll realise that the large trout is, in fact, a small salmon.

~ ~ ~

Dawn

~

JOHN MCINNES

In December 1991 and January 1992 there were just a few short fine spells to give a lift to an otherwise miserably wet trout fishing season. Nearly every day during them I was on the river before dawn.

Midsummer pre-dawn in the upper Manawatu Valley is surprisingly noisy. Two-, 3- and 4-wheel farm vehicles sputter and roar on their way to milking. Dogs bark, magpies caw, a bull bellows and late lambs bleat. That particular summer, at the river on the fine days, there was another quieter, more discrete sound: the 'ploph, plumph, plunkh' of trout at work—the dawn rise.

On Boxing Day I reached the grassy bank between the willows just as first feeble light began to flow. As I came through the trees, a wee bit later than I meant to, I found fish already feeding in my favourite early stretch. Because I'd realised the night before that mayflies were about, my cast was loaded with a pretty little artificial mayfly tied after the Dad's Favourite style—dark brown legs, grey wings, neatly marked body.

Wonderful to have mayflies again. They had been heavily outnumbered by caddis flies the few previous years. In fact I'd sometimes wondered if mayflies as we used to know them—big hatches which brought the river alive with trout—would ever appear again.

River banks just before still summer dawns are magic—soft and spooky. Nothing is defined. Nothing is coloured. Everything is indistinct and illusive. Stepping carefully, dressed in camouflage clothes and therefore virtually invisible against a grassy slope, even as the light increased, I snuck into place. The 'snuck' had to be done exceedingly slowly. Tripping over, getting the rod jammed or the net caught was only too easy. A consequent great commotion on the bank would likely scare away both the fish and the magic.

Still largely obscured by the dissolving dark, the rises weren't easy to see in swirly water where the foam line was wide and broken. At first I couldn't get a fly near a fish. But I've learnt that fish feeding in such a widely dispersed foam line move around a great deal, and that I should wait until one came within range. So when the rise forms began to track to my side and drift back down the current until they were just a little upstream and across from where I stood, I tried to settle down and fish as well as I possibly could.

The trouble is that I suffer stage fright—river bank fright. When I arrive around dawn and the fish are working, I get so excited that my heart pumps quickly and my skill sinks a notch or two. Therefore, like a runner under stress entering the final straight, I concentrated on form. Cast lightly. No line slam. Give enough slack to let the fly land and drift down the current without drag. Compensate even more than usual because I was casting from a raised bank.

Several fish were rising. They worked the laterally dispersed foam line back and forth, up and down. Must have used a lot of energy. But foam lines indicate currents carrying drifting food so I suppose the effort was worthwhile. I peered into the emerging light. Difficult fishing this. Trees right and left determined the angle at which I could cast. Prolific growth on the bank caught the fly if I let the backcast drop at all. It wasn't quite a steeple cast but the backcast certainly had to be thrown well up into the sky. Then, to shoot the line out under an overhang I had to suddenly crouch down and drop the wrist as the rod came forward.

'Oooh' I groaned to myself as I didn't get the line shoot quite right and the fly skidded across the water instead of falling neatly and softly. But wow. Fish! I saw him coming with his mouth open. He was chasing the skidder. Bang. He took. Snap! He turned over and went down. I flipped my wrist in the strike. He was on. Now came the difficult part. Between my grassy bank and the water surface stretched about 4 feet of heavily dewed, very slippery papa. I had to duck under one or two protruding willow branches and get down with the net. Doing so wasn't easy.

Once before here, at night, my feet had shot from under me and I'd ended in the water with the fish and had to swim a stroke or two before getting downstream far enough to touch bottom. Another time I fell and bruised my hip and it hurt for months. Great place to fish, though.

This time I did better. I use very strong nylon in the dark and this fish wasn't huge. I held tight, reached down with the long-handled landing net and managed to sink the rim in the water, shuffle the fish over it, then swing the net up the bank. Two and a half pounds.

Probably because of the gloom and the swirly water the other fish weren't scared. They continued to feed. Could I catch another? One for me and one for the farmer whose land I'd crossed. I washed the fly. Drying flies when there is a fair bit of moisture in the air and no sun is hard so I pushed the now wet but slime-clean fly into the silica gel granules which I carry in a little plastic pill bottle. Silica gel sucks up the water. Pretty useful. The fly came out looking like a snowflake. I let it stay like that for a minute or two then blew the granules away.

The hackles sat up as if newly minted and the fly was ready to go again.

I'd kept an eye on the water while drying the fly and now that the light had come I could see more easily. Three fish at least were in a rough sort of Indian file in the current yet moving a long way sideways. Sometimes they made just a bulge but sometimes I could see the snout and hear the jaws snap shut. The rise was well under way and mayflies were hatching at quite a rate. Ten minutes more and it would probably all be over.

Quickly I crept into position again. Once I'd started casting I kept the fly in the air, even though I had to dodge the trees and clumps of grass on every backcast. Then, when I saw a rise, I dropped the fly above and near the top edge of the rings in the hope that he'd come again, before he moved off across the river in search of a hatcher at the other side of the foam line. For a wee while nothing happened, except that every now and then the fly caught something on the bank, and I'd have to stop, rescue it and start again. Frustrating, but I knew that if I didn't control the frustration I'd not look like catching another fish. Agitation is no use. Needed are body stillness and soft hands.

Ah! There was a bulky rise, and this time with the line clear and controlled in the air, I shot the fly across. I could see better now as light began to hit the water. The fly fell just where I wanted it. Wuumph! Got him! This one felt heavy.

If the last one was difficult to land, this one was going to be an even tougher test. He turned and ran and I had no option but to let him go. Stout cast I might have, but I didn't want the hook to wrench out. I dipped the rod under overhanging branches in front and below me, ducked low, then half crawled under a tree to the grassy patch in the next tree-free gap downstream. The fish continued to pull across and down the river. He was heading for the log pool. Presumably he lived there and only came up into this run to feed.

I sat on my backside and slid down the papa feet first into waist-deep water. Oooch! Cold! But the river bed was solid, so I waded, then, when I reached the shallows, half ran after him with the rod now clear of willows and able to be held high. He was steaming down the ripple, the line feeling the pull of the current and the reel showing the backing. I clambered out onto the stony beach and stumbled on as fast as possible, winding in as I went. At last I gained line as we reached the quieter water of the log pool. Then there was not too much trouble. I hate playing a fish for a long time. Quickly I waded knee deep, let him come over the sunken net and lifted. Good one! Heavy. Four and a half pounds on the little spring balance. The farmer would be pleased. He had one of his daughters and some grandchildren with him for Christmas-New Year and I knew they all liked having a fish to eat. 'What a huge one,' they said when I gave it to them. 'We didn't know they were that big in our river.'

Great fishing, the summer dawn. Mystical, eerie, heart stopping. Big fish gulping flies on the surface. Magic. The wonder is that I always have the river entirely to myself. In the nearly 30 years I've fished the Manawatu, I've never seen another daybreak angler.

～ ～ ～

Fishing

~

JAMES NORCLIFFE

1

The diesel engine throbbed comfortingly as the launch eased its way out of the marina, under the coat-hanger-like footbridge and chugged quietly into the bay. The young man, standing in the stern, gazed around as the foreshore seemed to slide past and slowly recede. The hills were covered in deep green, the sky was blue, and the white buildings of the small town glittered in the morning sun.

Great day for you, Rob, cried a voice.

He looked over his shoulder, grinning, and nodding.

Great!

Rosie's mother grinned back. He felt something had been bestowed. She was a busy woman, that he'd already discovered, and that she should take time out to grin and pass the time of day was some sort of boon. Already she was efficiently unpacking an old chilly bin and sorting things out on a sort of workbench arrangement built into the port gunwale of the stern. He saw two or three large and very sharp-looking knives, and a plastic bag filled with something grey which shuddered with the vibration of the engine, now chugging faster and more loudly as the launch moved into the sound proper. Previously Min, as he'd been told to call her, had fished several large buckets overboard and half filled them with water. These were disposed in places around the deck as if they were sentries.

For the fish, Min had grunted, as she'd lugged them to their stations.

Rob wondered whether to take his jacket off or leave it on. The sun was warm but there was a coolish breeze off the sea. He looked back at the town across the diamond-flecked aquamarine water. Already it was shrinking considerably, embraced by the widening vee of the wake. He wondered whether he ought to join Rosie in the wheelhouse with her father, Ben, but he decided not to. They would have things to talk about, probably. He still felt something of an intruder when the three of them were together. Ben was slow and quiet, still in the process of summing Rob up. He decided to stay put. It was safer. Min, the little dynamo, was too busy to engage in conversation and so he didn't have the problem with her of trying to find some common ground beyond the existence of her daughter. Rosie.

A sudden banging sound made him look back at Min once again.

With one of the sharp knives she was chopping enthusiastically at strips of pinky grey flesh. An empty plastic bag flapped, pinioned under a ring of lead sinkers.

Catching his eye, Min grinned again. Just chopping up bait, she explained. Bit of squid. Don't want to waste good fishing time.

2

So what d'you reckon? asked Rosie, staring through the salt-stained window of the wheelhouse.

Could be all right, said her father, scratching at a small scab on his temple.

Rosie nodded.

We'll go up the channel, said her father. Found a good possie there last time.

Rosie glanced at him. He was talking about the fishing. She hadn't been. He caught her look and gave a small tight smile. He knew she hadn't been talking about the fishing.

3

Done a lot of fishing, then, Rob? Ben had asked the evening before.

Rob shook his head. Not really, he said. Just off the rocks and stuff. Sometimes go over to Lyttelton when I was a kid, you know.

Ben nodded. What's the weather like, Min? he shouted across to the dining room where the two women were still sitting at the table talking.

Rosie's father and Rob were in the lounge drinking beer. From his roly-poly build Rosie's father had obviously drunk quite a lot of beer. Min and Ben. Ben and Min. The names, to Rob, had seemed to belong to a comic duo. This impression had been confirmed earlier on when he'd met them for the first time. They were both small people, but Min was thin, wiry, with the air of a scurrying little bird, whereas Ben was rotund, slow, with a bush of white hair and a brick-red face. For the life of him, Rob could find no resemblance to Rosie in either of them. Perhaps she'd been a foundling. It was difficult to know, too, exactly how Rosie felt about her parents. She seemed easy enough with them, but rather neutral.

It's meant to be beautiful! Min called. Or so they said on the television.

Ben sipped thoughtfully at his beer.

Might take the boat out, then, he said. Introduce young Rob here to a few blue cod.

Rob glanced through to the dining room. The women had looked up. Rosie was smiling encouragingly at him, and Min was nodding enthusiastically. He understood he was to show keenness and gratitude.

Sounds wonderful, he said.

Right then, said Ben. Wonderful. Funny sort of a word to use. He looked thoughtfully at his empty glass. Again Rob understood. He stood up and fetched a beer bottle from the small coffee table and filled Ben's glass carefully.

In the background he could hear Min's laughter.

Getting him trained, already, Ben? she called.

4

When they'd climbed in the Mazda station-wagon for the short run to the marina Rob had hoped to sit beside Rosie in the back, but by some clever footwork he was too slow to comprehend Min had pre-empted him, and he had been left to sit beside Ben in the front.

You boys'll have lots to talk about, Min had cried.

Rob had doubted it. His usual conversational gambits dried in his mouth in the face of Ben's faraway silences.

As it happened, it had been Min who insisted on conversation from the back seat, while Ben concentrated entirely on the road.

And what do you do, then? she'd shouted. When you're not at the polytech, that is . . .

To avoid complications he and Rosie had agreed on a story that they'd met at the polytech where they were doing a business studies class together.

He works at the Farmers, Mum, Rosie had replied for him; then added a little crossly: I've told you that already.

Rob had had a panicky moment wondering what else Rosie had told her mother already.

He can speak for himself, can't he? Min had replied, equally crossly. The Farmers is a big place. He's a big boy. He can speak for himself, can't he?

Got far to go? Rob asked of Ben, vaguely irritated by the way Rosie and her mother were speaking of him in the third person.

Not far, Ben had grunted in reply, amiably enough. But he didn't elaborate.

So what do you do at the Farmers? Min had persisted.

He sells clothes, Rosie had replied.

Not lingerie, I hope, Min had laughed.

Rob had decided to risk humour.

Well, I do actually, he'd said. I'm a traveller in women's underwear . . . Ben had taken his eyes off the road just long enough to telegraph a look of scorn.

What was that? Min had asked, surprised.

It was a joke, Rob had capitulated. Just a joke.

He sells menswear, Mum. He's just been made a buyer, Rosie had explained.

Rob, sensing Rosie's disapproval, had been very relieved when shortly afterwards the car swayed off the road and down the steep entrance to the marina.

5

Min splashed her hands in one of the buckets of sea water then turned to Rob and said, Do something for me, Rob?

Rob nodded, pleased. He was beginning to feel a little useless, a spectator.

Pop down into the cabin, will you? The rods are down in the far corner. Bring four of them up, will you, and we'll set them up.

Rob climbed down the short companionway into the small cabin. The interior had a salty painty smell which was not unpleasant. There were benches that could serve as bunks, and an after-cabin with another couple of bunks. A sink-bench, fold-down table, shelves and cupboards. Everything was neat and ordered. A trifle miniaturised. Shipshape. Even the rods, when he found them, were arranged in order of height and each was lodged in its own bracket. There were eight or so. He selected four at random and unclipped them. The engine throbbed with a different sound down there and there was a slight movement which caused him to lurch as he walked. But not much. The sea was very calm and the boat was steady in the water.

Returning to Min with the rods he blinked in the bright sunshine.

Wonderful day, he said. Couldn't be better.

We love coming out in the boat, she said. Especially when there's plenty of fish.

Be good to get a few today, said Rob.

Min nodded. Thanks, she added, taking the proffered rods. Then: Oh, you forgot the sinkers and the hooks.

Rob felt a little rebuked and resented it. Was he a mind reader?

The large cupboard in the corner where the rods were, a red lunch box, said Min.

Rob returned to the cabin, found the old tin box and handed it to Min.

Ben always insists on taking the hooks and sinkers off the lines before we store them, Min explained. I'm not sure why. It's a bit of a fag getting them all ready again each time.

Rob couldn't think why, either.

Still it gives you something to do. He's very particular about things like that.

Very particular about most things, Rob thought, remembering the outstretched glass, the hands gripped rigorously at 10 to 3 on the wheel, the look of surprised scorn.

Want to put a few sinkers on? Min offered.

Another test. Rob shook his head. I'm not sure . . .

Hooks are easy, said Min. Here, I'll show you. The silly old bugger does let us leave the loops on.

Rob found it easy enough. He pushed the loops through the eye of the hooks and doubled them through. The hooks were surprisingly large.

Mind yourself when you put the bait on, said Min, handing him a handful of slippery squid pieces. You can do yourself a nasty injury. She laughed.

It's okay, said Rob.

All the same, he punctured the ball of his thumb a number of times with the sharp little points as he worked the bait through. He wanted to suck the thumb but the stink of squid was strong and unpleasant. Finally the job was done and he splashed his hands together in one of the buckets of sea water.

Blue cod, said Min. That's what we're after.

Rob breathed in. The smell of the sea and of the water on his hands with the faint after-pungency of the bait was almost refreshing.

Great, he said. Rosie and her dad . . .

They'll have a lot to say, said Min. He misses her.

Rob nodded.

Not far to the channel now, said Min. What about a cup of tea?

She left him and descended into the cabin, returning with some polythene cups and a thermos flask.

Hope you like milk and sugar, she said. It's easier if you don't have to bother about . . .

Rob, who didn't, shook his head. It doesn't matter, he said.

As soon as the sweet hot tea swirled into his mouth Rob regretted it. It wasn't the sweetness, or even the slight cheesiness of the milk, a taste he especially disliked: it was something emanating from the soft polythene cup itself. A vague oiliness of fish. A hint of diesel.

Cheers, said Min, raising her cup. I'll just take some to the others.

Rob raised his cup as well, a gagging almost overtaking him. O God, let me not be sick, he thought. The queasiness rose in him, and at the thought of sickness the motion of the boat seemed accentuated. The rolling. The rocking. As soon as Min was safely out of sight he tipped the fawn liquid overboard, swallowing, fighting back the panicky nausea. He felt a succession of hiccoughs born in his gut rise to the surface, and at the same time he was forced to swallow mouthful after mouthful of the watery saliva he knew preceded sickness.

Look! shouted a voice. Rosie's voice.

His head was down, his eyes closed. He could hear Rosie clumping along the narrow decking beside the wheelhouse. She jumped down beside him.

You all right?

He nodded, swallowing, attempting a small grin.

Fine.

You look a bit pale. Look, the ferry!

He followed her finger. Moving into the sound from the channel a way up ahead he could see the huge white shape of the inter-island ferry. It passed well in front of them and moved out into the deep water of the Queen Charlotte Sound proper, heading for Picton.

There was another clumping sound as Min rejoined them.

It'll get a bit bouncy when we fetch its wake, she said.

Soon the ferry passed them amidships, towering above them. Rob could see the passengers clearly on the decks. Some waved. For some obscure reason he felt a little superior as he waved back. He was glad of the diversion, however, and even enjoyed the wild rocking as they were caught in the bow waves of the huge vessel, bracing his feet widely apart for purchase as the launch swung up and down.

Min grinned at him. We'll make a sailor of you yet, she said.

Rob grinned. It's a great day, he said.

Finished your tea? asked Min. Want some more?

Rob shook his head. Even the suggestion wasn't enough to bring on a return of the nausea. It was going to be all right, he thought gratefully. And then he caught Rosie's curious gaze, and wondered what she was thinking. She wasn't to let him in, however, for she abruptly turned away and gave her attention to the rods stacked ready and waiting in a far corner. One by one she checked the baits, wrapping, folding, stitching the pieces of squid more tightly and securely onto the hooks.

6

It was very pleasant in the channel. Ben would shut the engine down off one of the little bays and the launch would gently drift in with the tide. Whenever the rocks loomed too closely they would reel in their lines and he would take the boat further out once more. If there hadn't been many bites he would veer off and find another little bay to drift towards.

With the engine shut down there was a much more intimate connection with the sea as it larruped and slapped around the boat which moved gently on its surface. Rob followed the sinker and the three gobbets of bait as the line was swallowed by the greenness of depth. Minuscule bubbles, moments of foam, white clouds.

Every so often he could feel a tickling vibration on the nylon as he sensed a fish investigating one of the baits, but rarely. Even more rarely came the insistent, desperate tugging signalling that he'd hooked something.

Not much doing, remarked Min.

Too many other buggers about, growled Ben. Look at them.

Rob looked about. Only then did he notice just how many other small launches, pleasure craft and runabouts were engaged in the same stately dance of drift and return. As they jockeyed for position Min would sometimes yell out to someone or other she knew, and then relay to the others some detail of medical history, or financial dealing, to give some dramatic context to the waving, smiling figures out of earshot.

Beer?

Rob took one, later another, of the cans Ben offered.

Occasionally, a fish would be caught, usually a blue cod, but invariably too small to be kept. It would be manoeuvred off the hook, grumbled at, then flung overboard again.

Bloody place is getting fished out, complained Min.

It doesn't matter, said Rob. It's just nice to be here.

Min glanced at him. You shouldn't be wearing those trousers. They're too good. You should've brought something older.

He didn't bring any, said Rosie.

I should have found some old ones of Ben's you could have put on, said Min.

Rob was about to laugh out loud at the stupid enormity of the suggestion, but just in time some instinct warned him Min was being perfectly serious, and he was able to avert the indiscretion.

It doesn't matter, he murmured.

Another beer? asked Ben.

Rob shook his head. No thanks, he said. Still got some.

I'll have one, Dad, said Rosie.

7

Rob was interested in an odd criss-crossing of type in the attitudes of Rosie's parents to fishing. Despite her busyness Min, it seemed, was the patient one. The usually phlegmatic Ben, on the other hand, was quick to judge whether or not a given spot was worth persevering with and was eager to get away if no bites were immediately forthcoming.

As it happened, Ben was the first to land a halfway decent fish. A blue cod. And shortly after he reeled in another. This time the fish was red.

Gurnard, cried Min. You beauty!

Rob didn't know whether Min was referring to Ben or the fish. He hoped it was the fish as it was certainly beautiful. Almost some sort of marine butterfly with its long tapering glittering red body and the huge dark pectoral fins like spotted wings. Ben wrenched the quivering body off the hook and flung it into the nearest bucket.

She'll do, he said.

Shortly afterwards Rosie reeled in another fish apparently worth keeping. Again Rob thought it beautiful. It was squatter than the gurnard and a rustier red with dark vertical stripes.

Maori chief, said Rosie. Do we keep it, Mum?

Better I suppose, said Min. They're not bad eating.

Rob admired the dexterous way Rosie held the fish and worked the hook out, before flinging it into the bucket.

Good girl, Rosemary, said Ben.

It occurred to Rob that he'd never heard either parent refer to Rosie as anything other than 'Rosemary'. Before this he'd never referred to her as anything other than 'Rosie'. It was a difficulty. When he was with the three of them both 'Rosie' and 'Rosemary' sounded awkward in his mouth.

It seemed they'd struck something of a lode. Two or three more of the striped red fish were pulled up. Then Rob felt a tickle that turned into an urgent tugging that wouldn't go away and he realised he'd hooked his first fish. He reeled the line in smoothly, the end of the rod dipping towards the water and twitching excitedly. As the nylon reached the surface he could see the dark red shape. Another Maori chief.

Pleased with himself, he was just reaching to grab the dripping dangling body as it flung itself about when he heard Ben's urgent shout: No!

What's that?

The rod was seized from him, and the fish laid on the deck. Ben's boot squelched on it and his knife hacked it off the hook. Before Rob's astonished eyes the twitching carcass was flicked over the side and into the sea where it sank down in a white belly-up parody of its recent ascent.

But?

Scorpion fish, grunted Ben. Hate those buggers. Won't have them on board.

Didn't you see the spines? asked Min. Nasty bloody brutes.

Rob shook his head.

Them and barracudas, said Ben. Won't have the buggers on board. Saw a barracuda take a bloke's finger off once. Silly bugger thought it'd been well and truly dead. Then snap! Proper bastards.

8

Later Rob found himself alone with Ben as they fished from the stern. The women had gone up to the bow.

It was a not entirely companionable silence, but Rob did not know how to break it. As it happened, Ben turned to him first. The man seemed to be struggling through his conversational gears. Rob waited.

You and Rosemary . . . Have you . . .

Rob felt a singing in his ears and reddened. He was convinced the man was going to take the direct approach: Have you slept together? Have you fucked? Or whatever bizarre circumlocution he could find.

But Ben finished rather lamely with: . . . made any, y'know, plans?

Rob felt relief. No, he said quickly. Oh, no. Just taking things as they come . . .

Rosie's father nodded. He too seemed relieved, and Rob felt somewhat discomfited by that.

Then Ben said, Getting close to those bloody rocks. Better pull out again. Actually, I think we'll call it a day. Been a bit of a waste of time today, hasn't it? Fished out.

9

They chugged down the sound in the late afternoon sun. Rosie was at the wheel, Rob standing at the stern, and Ben and Min were filleting the few fish they'd saved. Min cut off the heads and tails while Ben, with easy confident slices with one of the razor-sharp knives, peeled off the fillets.

Min threw the scraps of fish over the stern where they bobbed briefly in the wake before being seized by one of the myriad of screaming gulls greedily following them.

I hate those bastards, said Ben, looking back at them malevolently. Scavenging bloody freeloaders.

Rob, said Min grinning. Watch this!

Deftly, she tied a length of nylon to a chunk of fish, and tied another chunk of fish to the other end.

What are you doing?

Watch!

Then, swinging one end of the nylon round and round her head like a gaucho's bola, she flung it high astern. Rob watched with growing alarm as a pursuing gull seized one of the pieces of bait.

You little beauty! roared Ben, as animated as Rob had yet seen him.

Within moments the other piece of bait had been grabbed. Rob could only imagine the grim consequences as the two now attached birds were lost in the crowd of squawking gulls. He seemed to see an awkward plummeting dive from the higher bird, but could not be sure.

Jesus! he muttered.

Ben was grinning broadly. That'll teach the greedy buggers, he laughed.

Rob turned and left. He made his way to the wheelhouse. Rosie was rigid behind the wheel.

What's going on?

They're just gutting the fish, said Rob.

I ought to go and help, I suppose, said Rosie. Here have a go. Take the wheel.

Aw, no, said Rob, demurring. Rather not.

Don't be so bloody silly, said Rosie, grinning. The sound's miles wide, you idiot. Just keep us going straight ahead.

Rob nodded, and took the wheel. Rosie was right. The sound was spacious and all but empty in the late afternoon light. Alone now, he found the throbbing engine a comfort.

10

Rosie joined her parents in the stern.

Nice day, dear? asked Min.

Not bad, said Rosie.

Min began emptying the buckets over the side as Ben, who'd finished his work, showed Rose the rather small collection of white fillets laid out on the bench.

Not much of a catch, Rosemary, he said.

Rosie looked at her father and gave him a small smile. Not really, she said.

~ ~ ~

Hook Hours

~

Sue Harlen

For my father

I
— Fishing is
a matter
of hook hours —
you said and
cast your line
out to the
horizon.
We never
missed a break,
even trolled
the long wake
for kahawai
as we ran
the channel.

I learned to
read the lines,
to wait in
a half-dream
on the slack
tide for signs
of groper
mouthing the
bait to bite;
played line to
the big one
when it ran

deep to shake
the hook's grip.

Between us
we pulled in
more than our
share over
all the bright
lost seasons.
This summer
the tuna
are running
early, but
I have spent
my hook hours
casting the
past for you.

II
You never heard;
thought it was
just a sea-bird
calling as the hook
sank. You pulled
me in again
bleeding silver
on the end of
your green line.

My mouth is torn;
I'm the one
that got away.
I'm the one
that bit back —
remember that.
Pack up your
gear, old man,
the tide has turned.

You won't know me;
I have sung you
onto the rocks,
sung you
a slow drowning;
strapped to the mast
you won't get past,
I haven't finished
with you yet.

III

I knew it
was not true
when they said
how you died,
for I saw
you fight in
a black sea
and sink, full
fathom five,
anchored to
an ebb tide.

I have fished
at the head
of Pelorus;
my line dragging
too heavy
for the lead,
snagged in your
jawbone or
your cold, red
eye. Holding
onto you
my hands bled.

I do not
want to bait
the dead where

they wait far
back in the wake,
or turn in
their deep bed.

I have let
go of you
to the soft
swell. When you
dream a world
dream me well.

～ ～ ～

Three Days Nymphing

~

JOHN PARSONS

Staccato rattles of crackers and shrill screams of children punctuated the still Turangi evening. Over on the paddock, great tongues of flame from a huge bonfire leaped and smoked in the cleared centre of an audience of cars. The camp dog barked, bewildered by the noise. Down in the town, fire-engines and ambulances and police cars stood by, just in case.

The din wouldn't keep me awake. I was dog-tired with the exercise I'd had all afternoon. Ever since a quarter to one, when I hooked a fish in the Bridge Pool, I'd been on the move in or alongside the Tongariro, forging upstream, crossing rapids, fighting fish.

What a wonderful afternoon it had been, full of sunshine and suddenly flowering yellow broom; full of the rush of cloudy-green river, of chaffinches and fantails hawking flies, of upstream breezes just useful enough to spur the casting line.

The palm of my hand told the story. A list of times recalled the succession of fish. First, 10 minutes after getting into a vacant Bridge Pool on sudden impulse to nymph it up, I hooked a fish that came off. I fished up the rest of the pool almost to the bridge without another touch, then headed for the cabin that was to be my home for the next few days, and rapidly deposited food stores and sleeping-bag.

The next fish came at 2.45 a few metres up Waddell's. One more, at 3.45, towards the head of the run, took the nymph but came off. Then I'd reached the top, where 4 fish came in rapid succession, at 4.00, 4.10, 4.15 and 4.20. I landed the first two, fighting them out of the main rush of water into the only marginally quieter water at the side.

But I couldn't do the same for the 4.15 fish. It was a good heavy rainbow and it broke the 6-pound leader. I landed the 4.20 fish, then pushed on through the scrub to the rush of tumbling rapids above the Poutu Pool and fought my way across to fish the Breakaway from the true left bank.

The Breakaway was thoroughly frustrating. I connected satisfactorily with 3 fish, and briefly made acquaintance with two more. I've a sneaking feeling that one of the fish that came off was a brown, and was consequently annoyed. It seemed that all the fish in the pool were only halfheartedly responding.

The 6.10 and the 6.15 fish came off too. The last one, at 6.35, was a slab. Only two others of the afternoon's summer fish had been slabs. All the rest were good solid rainbows.

Going up the Boulevarde, intent as never before on landing a brown, I found pocket after pocket empty of fish. Even the first substantial holding-point returned me nothing. And the only places higher up, where fish finally did take, returned me only rainbows. Moderately well-mended kelts they were, and now and again a deep, thick, pretty fish of a pound and a half or so.

I half expected the disappointment of the Boulevarde because I hadn't raised a single fish in the Groynes—an extraordinary state of affairs. True, the Hydro proved moderately benevolent. First a small lively hen took the nymph, then a couple of tiddlers. Then I landed a reasonable fish, 3½ pounds or so, but nothing more. This perhaps wasn't too surprising since a downstreamer had just fished through the lie, hooking 3 fish, including the single silver hen of a couple of pounds or so which he cleaned and took away with him.

Absence of browns was a surprise. Normally, a Boulevarde excursion turns up one for me, rarely more. Today was tantalisingly odd. After yesterday's 11 hooked fish, I was fully expecting at least as strenuous a day. Maybe the weather wasn't as promising as it had first seemed. At 9.30 am shining cuckoos were welcoming the sun. But patches of thin cloud were straggling over from the west, and I remember half-thinking before I left the car that it might be prudent to stow the parka in the back of the fishing vest.

Imperceptibly, the clouds joined up. By 11.30 a smoky gloom covered the whole sky. Still the odd fish came at the nymph. I held one too hard, and the 5-pound nylon parted at the hook. Ten minutes later, fishing a replacement nymph, I was playing a very strong fish. I landed her eventually in the fastish water under the bank, and found I'd hooked her in the back. I took the nymph out, then saw that she had another in her lower jaw. It was the one I'd just lost. Had she gone for the second nymph automatically, then shied away, remembering, only to foul-hook herself?

After lunch back at the car I almost decided to head for Otamangakau, but tiny spots of rain appeared on the windscreen. Pihanga's wide brow frowned under mist, so I drove for the Red Hut Pool. I would fish Waddell's up again, then cross over to the Bypass and fish the Breakaway again from the other side. So far the tally was 6 fish hooked—or should it be 5, counting the twice-hooked hen as just one?

Well, I went up Waddell's and took a couple more, but that was all. Gentle rain was falling intermittently. Even at the top of the pool, alongside the rush of water, I couldn't raise a single fish.

Tired out, I reeled up and lay down at the edge of the lupins. Rain on my face woke me. I headed for the Bypass, crossed over at the Nursery, and plodded up the track for the Breakaway. I'd fish it from the other side again, I thought, and waded into position. My first cast travelled barely 5 metres when the indicator zoomed away upstream and a seemingly good fish whipped round and down.

The only trouble with fishing the Breakaway from the other side is that you're standing several metres away from shore in the usual skating rink of medium-bore Tongariro cannonballs. So I put pressure on and netted the long 3½-pound hen—which ought to have been at least 5 pounds—in midstream. Another one came and I netted that at the same spot. The next one came off. And that was Sunday.

And now the rain is really settling in. How lucky for the kids that they'd had such a fine evening last night for their fireworks.

Next day, masochist that I am, I went to Otamangakau.

Otamangakau is infuriating. Where were the fish today? I did know where one was, for half an hour or so. It was the only fish rising within a kilometre in any direction, and it rose on maybe 10 occasions, 3 of them so close to the end of my line that I was growing extremely nervous.

But no twitch of the chironomid pupa, no teasing wind-drifted navigation around, could concentrate the attention of that fish on the one chironomid it should have taken.

The trout was actually head-and-tailing. So I took off the sinking pupa and knotted on a lightweight No. 14 Sedge—the very fly that had taken my one and only lake fish from Otamangakau so far. That wonderful fish had weighed 8 pounds 2 ounces, and it came after dark, and I landed it in 5 minutes, much to my surprise.

But today's fish wasn't having any, so I swore at it and reeled up.

For Otamangakau, the weather was superb. Light westerly breezes came and went. Raggedy white and grey clouds patched the sky. Sunshine was on the water most of the time. Distantly, cock pheasants belched. Larks trilled overhead.

Should one fish the lee or windward shore at Otamangakau? Far away, out from the inlet canal mouth 3 black dots of fishermen were casting. They were at the windward end in some respects: hatching chironomids and sedge would perhaps be wind-drifted past the inlet canal. At least they had a trout, for towards the end of the morning, when they trudged back to their car, one of them walked down the boat ramp to wash the fish.

When you're casting south, as they had been, you don't see the magnificence of Tongariro and Ruapehu rising, snow-clad, into the clouds. From my side, before the cloud slowly began to thicken, I was always conscious of those two giants. The nearer slopes of Tongariro were dark brown and grey. Only a few gullies, spread like fingers from the flat tops, still carried snow. But the peaks behind were white and, round to the west, where Ruapehu peeped, the snow was thick, dazzling in the sun.

Although, for Otamangakau, the weather was unquestionably superb, the wind flowed fitfully quite the wrong way—the wrong way for me, that is. When I'm fishing the inlet canal I need a breeze upstream. Today's breeze was perfect at times, but always downstream. This meant that every cast was fished out too fast. Once the floating line bellied downstream, the breeze would force the nymph across and round at quite 4 times the pace of any natural insect. Conversely, a breeze coming upstream slows the drift, makes the nymph falter, gives it slight movement upstream when you gently check the line.

I even tried walking downstream to keep drag to the minimum, but eventually drag was set up, and any fish would have given the nymph a wide berth.

Casting upstream was fraught with distressing mental perils. A breeze on the right cheek is a wicked thing, and I always recall on those occasions how near I once was to burying a hook in my left eye. And if you're fishing the inlet waterway up, to make matters worse, the bank behind you rises up quite sharply and is armed with toetoe and suchlike trivia. And at your feet grow waist-high clumps of the true rush, those companies of slim green ramrods with knobby buttons welded to them near the top.

But it was a joy to be in thighboots after 2 days of chest-waders. In a way it was a day of rest, of fishing without the surge of powerful currents. And yet, at 5 o'clock, I was back among the cannonballs of the Tongariro, hoping I might yet get a fish that day.

I'd decided I would stick to thighboots and I only hoped I would remember my vulnerability if I hooked a good fish and had to chase off downstream after it.

Once again, and rather ominously, nothing stirred in the best of the Groynes. But first cast at the bottom of the Hydro I was into fish. By 6.30 I'd hooked 6 and landed 5, all well-mending kelts, and all of them taken on the *H. colonica* imitation.

Ghosts have been with me these past 3 days. Whenever a rare visit to the Poutu Pool takes me through the scrub surrounding the old Dreadnought, I always think of Zane Grey battling big rainbows there way back in 1926. Now, that famous Tongariro pool, that roaring surge of water against the Dreadnought bluff, where a dumbfounded Zane Grey fought 10-pound fish, is a waste of stones and pumice and scrub all round. The pool emptied in the raging flood of 1958, which took the river on a new course.

Today, if wooden bridge-planks endure for half a century, I may have walked where Grey walked, fearing for his life. Remember how one evening Hoka Downs led Grey, and Mitchell, and others of the party, through the bush to a steep drop leading down to the narrow bridge over the Poutu, on their way to the Dreadnought? Two stanchions stand on one bank at the point where surely the old bridge spanned the river. They are metal stanchions, possibly of recent origin, for some hundreds of metres away, abandoned perhaps as too heavy to shift further, a steel girder with metal uprights spaced along it lies rusting in the grass. Was this to have been a new Poutu footbridge? Near the stanchions, still sound, lie two old timber planks which would have been long enough between them to span the river.

Colin Hill was a far more likeable man than Grey could ever have been. From all accounts the American was a boor, no matter how well he wrote about fishing. So, as I trudged lonely ways from pool to pool today, I knew which ghost I would rather have had walking with me, along tracks gloriously hedged with yellow broom blossom from which rabbits and blackbirds and chaffinches and quail, and once a little grey warbler, scuttled off to deeper sanctuary.

The sorrowing for Colin is less now, but when I fish the Boulevarde I see him standing at the bottom pocket playing the two rainbows he landed there while I watched from the bank.

And now the kowhai is in bloom over that secret piece of water higher up. Colin died in May, so he never saw the blossom on the tree for which he named that particular new hole we found, where each of us hooked and lost a big fish, twice, and were certain it was the same one, a big brown for sure.

Today was a thighboots day again. I wasn't going to tramp 3 kilometres to the Whitikau in chest-waders, and I didn't fancy wearing ordinary shoes and carrying the waders slung round my neck.

Broom frothed yellow everywhere, an astounding gala performance that never fails to impress, year after year. And the day seemed good: sunny, cool yet at 8.30, but clear except for a few ragged clouds. But the water was faintly milky-green. The high cliff across the Whitikau Pool was cheerful with sparrow and starlings nesting, and once two paradise duck landed briefly up there.

Only one fish came to the nymph, and broke off again. Maybe the sun hadn't been long enough on the water. So I beat a retreat to Harry's Rock, which had been warming in the sun for some hours. The reach above it yielded, wonder of wonders, two good fish, one of which I kept.

Time was running out. My 3 days were almost up. After an early quick lunch back at the car I went fairly rapidly up Boulder Reach, found the water in good condition, and landed 4 fish, one of which I kept. Later, a last fling in the Hydro produced another 4 fish, all of which went back again. And that was that.

Not counting the occasional small fish, I'd hooked 38 fish in a little over 3 days' fishing with the nymph. Only 2 had been worthy enough to keep of those I'd landed, and all the rest had gone back again.

Maybe some of them would have appointments with me again? Provided they were deep, gleaming, grey and silver running fish by then, I wouldn't mind at all.

~ ~ ~

Beneath the Falls

~

BRIAN TURNER

You never take the same path twice
to the pool beneath the falls. Twigs
snap under your feet, leaves swish
as you push through overhanging foliage.
On the far side a tapestry of moss
hangs from a mantel of chocolaty earth;
stones like beans gleam
along the edge of the stream
where sunshine strikes them
and glances off the water that's
painted glossy green by the willows.

There's a big trout idling,
hanging to the left of foam
like a line of marshmallows
drifting, veering. It's feeding:
its white mouth opens and closes
periodically
as it *chasses* in the current.

You begin to strip line
from the reel, measure the distance.
You have the heart
but it's skill you need,
and nerve. The fish rises
and falls silhouetted against a marbly
white stone. You aim to lay,
not lash, line on the water,
and every sound rod and line makes
is meant to syncopate,
find a rhythm that accentuates

the sounds of air,
the flow of water.
The fish rises again
with a slow insolence . . .
but you strike too soon
and you're left
with a bare marbly memorial
and the insouciant rush
of water foaming from the falls.

~ ~ ~

Waiariki

~

PATRICIA GRACE

When we were little boys we often used to go around the beach for kai moana. And when we reached the place where the rocks were we'd always put our kits down on the sand and mimi on them so the shellfish would be plentiful.

Whenever the tides were good we would get our kits and sugar-bags and knives ready, then go up at the back of our place to catch the horses—Blue Pony, Punch, Creamy and Crawford. And people who lived inland would ring and ask us about the tides. 'He aha te tai?' they'd ask over the phone—'What time's the tide?' and we'd tell them. All morning the phone would ring; 'He aha te tai? He aha te tai?'

And on those days there would be crowds of us going round the beach on horses with our kits and knives, and when we arrived at the place for gathering shellfish we boys would mimi on kits and sugar-bags then wash them in the salt water, all of us hoping for plenty of kai moana to take home.

We never thought much about the quiet beauty of the place where we lived then. Not in the way I have thought about it since. I have many times wished I could be there, living again in our house overlooking the long curve of beach and the wide expanse of sea. We could climb up through the plantation behind our place to the clearings at the top and look away out for miles, and could feel as free as the seagulls that hung on the wind above the water. It was from this hill that I once saw a whale out off the point, sending up plumes of spray as it travelled out to the deep. And on another occasion from the same hill, we watched the American fleet go by, all the ships fully lit, moving quietly past in the dusk.

If we went down the gully and up on the hills at the left we could look back to where our old house had been, then down to the present dwelling with all the flower gardens which kept us busy all year round. One would have thought that with vegetable gardens to tend, our parents would not have had time for flowers, but flowers, shrubs and trees we had in abundance, and looking down from the hills, or from the beach below, the area round the house was always a mass of colour. But it is now, looking back, that I appreciate this more.

The bird tree was our favourite, with its scarlet flowers like red birds flying.

Then there were the hibiscus of many different colours, the coral tree, kaka beak, and many varieties of coloured manuka and broom. And there was a big old rata under which one of our brothers was born, and named Rata for the tree.

In front of the house at the end of the lawn was a bank where scores of coloured cinerarias, black-eyed Susans, and ice plants grew, and beyond there was the summer house that my fathers and brothers built before I was born. This was where my father had all his hanging baskets crowded with ferns and flowers.

When I first left there to go away to school, and when I first realised what other people had in the way of money and possessions, I used to think how poor we children were. I used to think about it and feel ashamed that our patched clothing, much of it army surplus, was the best we had. And felt ashamed that the shoes that had been bought for me for high school were my first and only pair. It wasn't until many years later that I realised that we had many of the good things, and all the necessary things of life.

There were 10 of us living in the house at the time I remember, but there were older children who had married and gone away. Seventeen children my parents had altogether, though not all lived. I can remember the day my youngest sister and her twin were born. Our mother had been away at one of the top gardens getting puha, and on our way home from school we could see her coming down the track on Crawford. And our father was standing by the gate with his hands on his hips, shaking his head.

'That one riding on a horse,' he was saying. 'That one riding on a horse.'

And Mum got down off the horse when she got home and said, 'Oh Daddy, I was hungry for puha.' Then she began walking round and round the house, pressing her hands into her sides, pressing her hands. Later she went to bed and Dad delivered the girl.

My big sister Ngahuia brought the new little sister Maurea out into the kitchen where it was warm and began washing her. Then Mum called out to Dad that there was another baby and at first he thought it was all teka. He thought she was teasing because he had growled about her riding on the horse. But when he went to her he knew she wasn't playing after all and went to help, but the boy was stillborn. Mum was sad then because she had been riding on the horse so close to her time, but my father was good to her and said no, it was because the boy was too small. They took the tiny body up to where the old place had been, and buried it there with the other babies that had not lived.

Maurea was never very strong and on most nights we went to sleep listening to the harsh sound of her coughing. That was until she was about 5 years old. Then our parents took her to an old aunt of ours who knew about sicknesses, and the old aunt pushed her long forefinger down our sister's throat and hooked out lump after lump of hard knotted phlegm. Maurea was much better from then on though still prone to chest complaints and has never been sturdy like the rest of us.

There were three different places we went for kai moana. The first, about a mile round the beach, called Huapapa, was a place of small lagoons and rock pools. The rocks here were large and flat and extended well out into the sea. This was a good place for kina and paua and pupu. We would ride the horses out as far as we could and tether them to a rock. They would stand there in the sun and go to sleep. To get kina we would go out to where the small waves were breaking, in water about knee deep. We'd peer into the water, turning the flat stones over, and it wouldn't take long to fill a sugar-bag with kina. The paua were there too, as well as in the rock pools further towards shore. The younger children, who were not old enough to stand in the deeper water and not strong enough to turn the big rocks for paua and kina, would look about in the rock pools for pupu, each one of them hoping to find the biggest and the best.

The next place, Karekare, further round the beach, was also a good place for shellfish, but the reason we liked to go there was that there was a small lagoon with a narrow inlet, which was completely cut off from the sea at low tide. Often at low tide there were fish trapped there in the lagoon. And we children would all stand around the edge of the lagoon and throw rocks at the fish.

'Ana! Ana!' we'd yell.

'Patua! Patua!' hurling the stones into the water. And usually there would be at least one fish floating belly up in the lagoon by the time we'd finished. Whoever jumped in first and grabbed it would keep it and take it home.

One day after a week of rain we arrived at Karekare to find the water in the lagoon brown and murky, and even before we got down from the horses we could see two dozen or more fins circling, breaking the surface of the water. We all got off the horses and ran out over the rocks calling, 'Mango, mango', and scrambled everywhere looking for rocks and stones to throw. But my father came out and told us to put the rocks down. Then he walked out into the lagoon and began reaching into the water. Suddenly he threw his arms up, and there was a shower of water, and a shark came spinning through the air, 'Mango, mango', way up over our heads with its white belly glistening and large drops of water raining all over us. 'Mango, mango,' we shouted. Then—smack! It landed threshing on the rocks behind us. So we hit it on the head with a stone to make sure of it, and turned to watch again. My father caught 10 sharks this way, grabbing their tails and sending them arcing out over our heads to the rocks behind, with us all watching and shouting out 'Mango, mango', yelling and jumping about on the rocks.

The other place, Waiariki, is very special to me. Special because it carries my name which is a very old name and belonged to my grandfather and to others before him as well. It is a gentle quiet place where the lagoons are always clear and the brown rocks stand bright and sharp against the sky. This was a good place for crayfish and agar. Mum was the one who usually went diving for crayfish, ruku koura. She would walk out into the sea fully clothed and lean down into the water, reaching into the rock holes and under the shelves of rock for the koura. Sometimes she would completely submerge, and sometimes we would see just a little bit of face where her mouth was, sitting on top of the sea.

The rest of us would feel round in the lagoons for agar. Rimurimu we called it. For the coarse agar we would need to go out to where there was some turbulence in the water, to pluck the hard strands from the rocks. But the finer rimurimu was in the still parts of the lagoons and we would feel round for it with our feet and hands, and pick it and put it into our sugar-bags.

When our bags were full we would take the agar ashore and spread it on the sand to dry. Then we'd put it all into a big bale and tramp it down. We had a big frame of timber to hold the bale, and our own stencil to label it with. I don't know how much we were paid for a bale in those days. But I do remember once, after one of the cheques had arrived, my father went to town and came home in a taxi with a rocking-horse and two guitars. He handed me one of the guitars and I tuned it up and strummed on it, and I remember thinking it was the most beautiful sound I ever heard.

And another time my father brought home a radio, and after that our neighbours and relations used to come every week to listen to *Gentleman Rider* or the *Hit Parade*. And when the boxing or wrestling was on people would come from everywhere. We'd all squeeze into our kitchen and turn the radio up as loud as it would go. On the morning after the fights we boys would go down to the beach and find thick strands of bull kelp and make our own boxing belts and organise our own boxing or wrestling tournaments on the sand.

The horses were very useful to us then. They were of more use to us than a car or truck would have been besides using them for excursions round the beach we used them for everyday work, and when the rain came and flooded the creek our horses were the only means we had of getting to town. All of our wood for the range was brought down from the hills by the horses too.

On the days when we were to go for firewood we boys would go up back before breakfast and bring the horses down, and after breakfast we'd prepare the horses for the day's work. Dad would sort out all the collars and chains, and we'd go out into the yard, put the collars on the horses, and hook the long coils of chain onto the hames. Then we'd get together the axes and slashers and start out down and across the creek, and go up onto the scrub-covered hills about a mile from the house.

It was always the younger boys' job to trim the leaves and side branches from the felled manuka and stack the wood on to the track ready to be chained into loads for the horses to pull. One of the older boys who had been chopping would come down and wrap the short chains round the stacks, then hook the long chains from either side of the horses' collars on to each side of the load.

Once when I was about 9 years old my father and mother were at the bottom of the hill stacking the wood into cords—we were selling wood then—for the trucks to come and take away to town. My older brothers were chopping and stacking at the top of the hill and my sisters and I were taking the horses down with the loads. I was on my way up the hill on Blue Pony and my sister was at the top hitching a load to Punch, who was a good willing horse but very shy. Erana accidentally bumped the chain spreader against Punch's leg and away he went. I saw Punch coming, bolting towards me with the chains flying, but it was too late to do anything. Punch knocked Blue Pony down, and I went hurtling out over the bank like Dad's mango thrown out of the lagoon.

I landed in scrub and fern and wasn't hurt. Everyone came running to look at me, but I got up laughing, and I remember my father saying, 'E tama, that one flying!' Then he went off to rescue Punch who was by then caught up in one of the fences by his chains.

On warm nights we used to like to go fishing for shark from the beach, Mangoingoi. We'd go down to the beach with our lines and bait and light a big fire there, and on some nights, especially when the sea was muddy after rain and we knew the sharks would be feeding close to the shore, there would be people spread out all along the beach, and 4 or 5 fires burning and cracking in the night.

We always used crayfish for bait, and because crayfish flesh is so soft we would bind it to our hooks with light flour-bag string. Then we would tie the ends of our lines to a log and prepare the remainder so that the full length of it would be used once it was thrown. We'd walk out into the sea then, twirling the end of the line with the hooks and horseshoe on it, faster and faster, then let it go. And the line would go zipping out over the sea, and sometimes by the fire's light we'd see the splash out off shore, where the horseshoe sinker entered the water.

We waited after that, setting up on the beach with our lines tied to our wrists. We'd talk, or sometimes sleep, and after a long while, usually an hour or more, someone's line would shoot away with shark.

'Mango, mango!'

'Aii he mango!'

And we would all tie our lines and go running to the water's edge, 'Mango, mango', to watch the shark being pulled in with its tail flapping and water splashing everywhere.

Mum used to cut the shark into thick pieces and boil it, then skin it. Then she'd put it into a pan to cook with onions, and we'd eat till we were groaning. Sometimes we would hang strips of shark flesh on the line to dry, and when this had dried out we would put it in the embers of our outside fire to cook. There was one teacher at school who used to get annoyed when we'd been eating dried shark at lunchtime. He'd march around the classroom flinging the windows open and saying, 'You kids have been eating shark again. You pong.' And we'd sniff around at each other wondering what all the fuss was about.

Dad used to hang the shark liver on the line too, and let the oil drip into the stomach bag. Then he'd put the oil in a bottle and save it to treat the saddles and bridles with.

I went back to the old place last summer and took my wife and children with me for a holiday. I wanted them to know the quiet. I wanted them to enjoy the peace, and to do the things we used to do.

In most ways the holiday was all I hoped it would be. My parents still live there in much the same way as before, even though the house seems somewhat empty now with only the two of them and two grandsons living there. Most of the other families have moved away. The vegetable gardens are not as extensive now because there is not the need, but flowers and trees are as abundant as ever, and the summer house is still there with my father's ferns flourishing and the begonias blooming.

Electricity hasn't reach that far yet, so it is still necessary for the old people to bring the wood down from the hills, and I don't like to think of them doing this on their own with only two small boys to help.

My wife and children had a good holiday. We spent two days getting firewood so that there would be plenty there after we had gone. Punch, Blue Pony, Creamy and Crawford are all dead now, and the two horses that they use are getting old too. There are other younger horses on the hills, but with no one to break them in they are completely wild.

I took my family up on the hills and we sat looking out over the sea. I told them about the whale I had once seen out past the point, and about the American fleet, all lit, going silently by.

And one night I took them down to the beach fishing, Mangoingoi. We caught a little shark too, and Mum cooked it for us in the old way and my father hung strips of it to dry and caught the oil in the stomach bag for the bridles and saddles.

Another day we all went round the beach for kai moana and, although the tides were good and the weather perfect, we were the only ones there on the beach that day. We visited all the favourite places and took something from each. And when we went to Waiariki, which even now I think of as my own special place, I told my children its name, and that it was special to me because I had that name and so had others before me. And my little boy said to me, 'Dad, why can't we stay here forever?' because he has the name as well.

But when we arrived at the first place with our knives and bags and kits and dismounted from the horses, and looked out over the flat rocks of Huapapa which is the best place for kai moana, I felt an excitement in me. I wanted to reap in abundance. I wanted to fill the kits full of good food from the sea. And then, I wanted to tell my children to put their kits down on the sand and mimi on them so that we would find plenty of good kai moana to take home. I wanted to say this to them but I didn't. I didn't because I knew they would think it unclean to mimi on their kits, and I knew they would think it foolish to believe that, by so doing, their kits would be more full of sea food than if they hadn't.

And when we left the rocks with our kits only half filled I felt regret deep in me. I don't mean that I thought it was because of my children not christening their kits as we stood on the beach that we were unable to fill our bags that day. There are several reasons, all of them scientific, why the shellfish beds are depleted. And for the few people living there now, there is still enough.

No. My regret came partly in the knowledge that we could not have the old days back again. We cannot have the simple things. I cannot have them for my children and we cannot have full kits any more. And there was regret in me too for the passing of innocence for that which made me unable to say to my children, 'Put your kits on the sand, little ones. Mimi on your kits and then wash them in the sea. Then we will find plenty. There will be plenty of good kai moana in the sea and your kits will be always full.'

～ ～ ～

The Fisherman

~

JAMES K. BAXTER

Between the day and evening
I fish from Barney's rock,
And watch the weedy channels fill
And hear the small waves knock,
And feel below their ledge's roof
The tugging greenbone flock.

When spiring seabirds mingle
Between the wave and sky,
The ka'wai chase the herrings in
Like soldiers dressed to die,
And on the beach for hands to pick
In flapping shoals they lie.

Upon an army pension
It suits a single man
To take from the sea's full cupboard
Whatever food he can.
The wound I got at Passchendaele
Throbs with the dying sun.

While loud across the sandhills
Clangs out the Sunday bell
I drop my line and sinker down
Through the weed-fronded swell,
And what I see there after dark
Let the blind wave tell.

~ ~ ~

The Sea off Westport

~

PETER HAWES

Royce

Royce Rowland was a 17-year-old sexual and social reprobate who had been sent to sea with a tough skipper in an effort to straighten him out. The consequences are Ulyssesian . . .

'We have 4 deaths a year in the sea off Westport,' said Bob Cobb.

It was the first thing he'd said.

Royce'd met Bob Cobb in the pub a few times but never really sat down and chewed the fat with him. Never actually said a word to him if truth be told, though Bob'd said a few to him, like 'Get outa the fucking way, kid.'

But even that was enough for you to say to your mates, 'I was chatting to Bob Cobb at the Albion the other night . . .' Was a legend in the district, was Bob.

One thing he was famous for was the day Buller played Canterbury on the Square, and Bob marked Alister Hopkinson the All Black. When Hoppy jumped for the ball in the first line-out, *pow*! By halfway through the second half they had to take him off; Bob had rendered him to pulp.

It was inspirational for the district, what Bob achieved that day—a minor union showing those up-themselves Canterbury buggers what it could bloody-well do . . . Mind you, the score was 76 nil to Canterbury.

The other crewman, Des Moody, was a tall, droop-eyed bloke with Popeye forearms and curly brownish hair that started a couple of inches further back on his head than you'd expect. It sort of went straight up, an inch or so, like a frizzy cliff. Royce'd seen him around from time to time.

Des didn't say anything when he came aboard a few minutes after them, just nodded, then went down this tight little wooden ladder at the front of the shed on the deck and disappeared. There was a vapour trail of booze behind him.

Bob Cobb had turned up 20 minutes late, after warning Royce the night before. 'Turn up after 5.15, boy, and we'll have gone. You're never late at sea.'

Royce—up since 4, on the wharf by 5—had waited, huddled in the shelter of a deserted Marine Department all-night surveillance post, hearing monstrous eels in the purple waters of the lagoon. They clucked under the piles of the wharf with the same sound as his grandfather made drinking tea.

He stood there, freezing his ass off and wondering if he'd dreamt that he was supposed to be here, till Bob Cobb turned up in a Bedford van with 4 hot loaves of white bread and a big plastic bag that he thrust at Royce. 'Maggot packs. Put them in the fridge when we get on board.' Frozen pies, hard as dominoes.

They climbed down this incredibly steep ladder that seemed to go on forever. He only knew he was getting somewhere by this big slab of blackness above him that blocked out more and more stars until, by the time he felt the side of the boat, half the sky was gone. It was the wharf, towering above him.

From the deck he could see little moonlit waves licking at the big, weedy piles and making the noise he'd thought was eels.

Bob Cobb did a fart that lasted about as long as the bloody national anthem while he unlocked a door in this sort of shed sort of cabin on the deck of the boat. He went in, and put a light on which only just singed the darkness.

Royce followed, put the pies in the fridge then hung around inside while Bob did irritably silent, purposeful houseworky things for ages. That's when Des Moody arrived and went down the ladder. Eventually Bob turned to Royce.

'What's that?' he said, nodding at the plastic bag Royce had brought from home.

'Sandwiches. My mum made them. They're for all of us.'

'What's in them?'

'Some are egg, some are banana.'

'Christ!' Bob Cobb ripped the plastic bag from him, went to the door and biffed the bag into the black cavern of the under-wharf. It landed with a thwack that made an echo.

'I should've known,' he snarled when he got back. 'You're a bloody Jonah already, boy, you know that? You don't bring bananas on a boat! Bananas are bad luck, okay?' Bob Cobb was glaring at him, from almost exactly Royce's own height. 'Now,' he purred, 'the grommet's job is to look after the skipper. You're the grommet, I'm the skipper. The first thing you do is you make the skipper a cuppa tea. There's the stove, get on with it.'

Then Bob marched off to the front of the shed and fiddled with electronic things. Some dials began glowing electric green.

From where Royce was standing, the cabin-shed-thing was a kitchen.

Behind him was the back door. Just before you went out, the kitchen turned into a bathroom, because there was a shower sticking out the side of the wall.

Where Bob was working was probably the bridge. He jabbed a switch down, pushed a button—and suddenly the boat was throbbing. That, it would seem, was all it took to make a fishing boat go.

'What sort of stove is it?' asked Royce.

'Diesel,' said Bob Cobb. 'And you don't know how to work it, do you?'

'No.'

You'd expect him to come jack-booting down the shed, glowing with bad temper—after all, not knowing diesel must be as bad as on-board bananas—but he just twiddled distractedly with knobs and said. 'You do that. And notice there's a clamp across the top of the stove. You push it tight up against the kettle, right?' The kettle was clattering to the movement of the engine.

'Yeah. I think so.'

'Do it.'

Royce did it. The clattering stopped.

'That's how you cook at sea.'

Bob Cobb went back out into the darkness beyond the bathroom door and threw ropes around.

When he came back inside he walked past Royce to the steering wheel saying, 'When you pick something up in a boat, you put it down exactly where it was, right? To the inch. You get so that you can put your hand on anything you want, blindfolded, right? So while you're waiting for that fucking water to boil, get memorising everything in the galley.'

'Galley?'

'Kitchen.'

'What do you call this . . . space we're in?'

'What?'

'You know, everything under this roof.'

You call it the wheelhouse, you dopey prick.'

'Right.'

'Because that's what it fuckingwell is.'

He hadn't noticed that they were moving away from the wharf. He did now. He could see the sheen of the moon on the dark water. Holy shite, he was off to sea—with a madman who hated him and a drunk, sleeping it off downstairs.

'What do you call the bit down there that Des is in?'

'You call it the fo'c'sle. You sleep there. Your bunk is on the port side. We're going nor' nor'east this trip, so that's the side that the seas will hit. Des will logically have taken the other.' He made another silence, then he said, 'The one across the boat, at this end of the fo'c'sle, is called the athwart bunk. That's mine. Raquel Welch, above the bunk, belongs to me and you don't even look at her.'

He was standing at the steering wheel looking out the window at two little red lights, one on top of the other, hiccuping on and off. He was steering towards them.

'When we come back, you'll steer this boat over the bar. Everyone on my crew can steer this boat. That way if I break my leg and Des is lost overboard, you can get me home. Start learning the compass as soon as you can.'

The kettle boiled. Royce took a semi-clean metal cup from a clever little cupholder in the wall and put it on the table. When Bob Cobb spoke, he did so without looking round.

'When you pour the tea, don't put the cup down. When you pour the milk, keep the cup and the bottle in your hands. One milk, two sugars. Have one yourself.'

They'd turned out of the floating basin into the main river. Royce now realised the red lights were on the left-hand wall of the tip head, a mile or so ahead, and that there were two green lights flipping on and off also, on the right-hand wall. Between them was the bar.

Beyond it was the sea off Westport.

He gave Bob his tea, took up his own and slunk out the back door.

The moon was still there, bright as tin, in the shape of a big sliver of toenail. A billion stars. A shooting one! That was supposed to be good luck. Yeah, and pull the other one.

Diesel smoke from their funnel drifted against the stars like nimbus cloud.

At least he knew his clouds. He'd give Bob Cobb a demonstration of his cloud knowledge, first chance he got. Bastard. He went inside.

'Tea's not bad,' said Bob. 'Better than that last deckhand of mine. Lazy bugger shakes the bag 3 times—maiden's water—then throws cow at it.'

Royce's little heart sang at the fulsome compliment.

A line of quivering moonlight confronted them just beyond the twitching red and green lights. It was a moving wall, seemingly as high as the walls of the tip head on either side of it.

'That's the bar,' said Bob Cobb quietly. 'I've crossed that mother four hundred times and I've nearly shit myself every time.'

They sailed quietly towards it. The moonlight glimmered on it like teeth in a phosphorescent smile.

Then they hit it. The boat shuddered, stalled, groaned and seemed to skid backwards. 'Oh God!' thought Royce's mind. His legs sagged as if gravity had doubled under him, and, worse, was dragging at his bowels. So powerful was the suction of gravity that he clanged his bum-hole shut in desperation, and just in time.

The moment passed. They popped unnaturally forward, like something spat out, and they were over the bar. Royce had nearly shit himself for the first time.

He gave a sigh which he heard echoed gently by Bob Cobb. The *Aurora* was now in swell, and seemed to be nodding its head up and down in delight. 'Yeeha, beat the fucker yet again!'

'Congratulations,' said Bob Cobb.

'Thanks,' said Royce.

Somehow, something had just changed. He would never be the same again.

They turned right (starboard) and headed (there it was, gyrating on the illuminated compass drum beside him) nor' nor'east.

Onion skins of darkness shed from the sky until the morning started to glow through the thinness. 'You play good rugby,' said Bob Cobb. 'I've seen you. You're fast.'

'I've done 11.4 for the hundred metres.'

'Ever had knee problems?'

'No. Not really.'

'Not lost any cartilage?'

'No.'

'You need good legs on a boat. Good knees.'

'Mine are all right.'

'You drive a boat by the soles of your feet, the arse of your pants and the strength of your knees.'

'Right.'

'This boat does 7 knots. It travels 7 miles in an hour. How fast is that?'

'Oh . . . that's 7 miles an hour.'

'Brilliant. We're going 18 miles out, how long will that take us?'

'Oh . . . bit over two and a half hours.'

'Brilliant. Go to bed for two and a half hours. Then be back up here for shooting the gear.'

'Right.'

'What does shooting the gear mean?'

'Um . . . I don't know.'

'It means putting the net out, you ignorant prick! If you don't know something, ask. When you're told, don't ask again.'

'Right.' Christ.

'Now fuck off and get some kip.'

Royce headed down into the stale depths that contained Des Moody.

'By the way, port's your left,' said Bob.

Royce looked up from the narrow ladder. Bob's face glowed a dreadful green in the light of the navigational instruments, but he seemed to be almost smiling. 'Thought I'd better tell you that; dunno what Des is into these days. Hee hee.'

The bunks were on the same slant as the prow. He was the prow. His head and Des's—6 inches apart—were pointing nor' nor'east, the width of the hull from the sea. Des's feet, to his starboard, were pointing south-east. His were pointing due south. Together they formed an arrow, pointing out into the sea off Westport.

When he got up, so had the sun. Westport had gone. So had Mount Rochfort. So had New Zealand. The world was made of big hunchbacked waves like whales diving.

Bob was out the front, standing by a winch, looking backwards down the boat. 'Get your fucking head outa the way, you're blocking my view.'

As Royce turned towards the galley he could see what Bob was seeing. He was looking through the wheelhouse, out the back windows to Des. Royce felt a hum. The big black wire that stretched from the winch to the back of the boat was moving. So was the one on the other side. You could only tell by the faint, oily noise.

Des was hooking a chain to a big tabletop of metal that stuck out from the side of the boat. He wrenched it somehow, and it fell into the sea. He went to the other side and wrenched another tabletop.

The tabletops sank, the black wires spread, the point they had formed in the boat's wake now widened into a V.

'We'll be shooting the gear three times today,' said Bob, 'three-and-a-half-hour drags. Tomorrow you'll be doing what Des's doing.'

'What are those things Des just biffed over?'

'Doors. They spread the net. We've got a 32-foot spread.'

'Without sounding dumb, where's the net?'

Bob Cobb's face puffed up with redness. 'You can't not sound dumb saying things like that, you dopey prick. The net's already out! Eighty yards behind us. See those birds? They're catching bits of junk that's floating up from the last drag. Jeesus! "Without sounding dumb." Spare me.' He was amazedly angry, but sort of looking as if he was enjoying it.

Seemed that was all there was to it. The gear had been shot. Des walked back up the deck towards them. He watched the black wire as if reading it, then leant on the rail beside Royce. Funny, he could make you nervous without saying anything. It was just there was something inside him vibrating about as fast as a bee's wing. You could feel it.

Royce's attention had been drawn to these amazing birds that scudded across the water so low they sometimes dipped their beaks into it, scribbling lines on the top of the sea. Then they'd swoop upwards, stall, and dive straight down into the water. He supposed they were catching fish though they never seemed to have one in their beaks when they came up. Maybe they ate them underwater.

'Gannets,' said Des.

'Know how you catch a gannet?' called Bob from the winch.

'No.'

'Nail a herring to a piece of plywood, throw it into the sea.'

Des

Something that Des would never admit in a million years is that he feels sorry for the fish. All those years in the sea off Westport and he still hates to see people like Bob booting the poor bastards round the deck, letting the little ones pant to death when they could have been biffed back in time to live.

Well, it's all about to happen again. The warps are humming and shedding earrings of water, the doors are wedged back in the bulwarks. Birds have turned up in their millions as usual—the wisdom is they know from the gear change of the boat's engine when a haul is coming up. He unclips the lazy wire from the second door, lowers the scuppers so the fish can't defect back into the sea from the deck and clips the net-roller rope on with a C link.

The bridles come up.

'What's that big netting for, Des? Anything but a whale would get through that.'

It is the kid, standing out of the way in the new semi-built dunny unit.

'It's called the sweep,' calls Des, 'acts like a sheep dog. Sort of herds the fish into the net. Mesh'll get smaller soon—they call that part the bunt.'

'Bunts the fish into the net?'

'You got it.'

The floats appear, and behind them, the net.

'Christ, it looks like a massive big red whale!' The kid is gawping at the hissing net that has lurkingly surfaced behind them.

Bob cuts the engine, the boat wallows and the kid is jerked out of the dunny unit by the new gravity. That unit has been semi-built for nigh on 10 years now, by Des's recollection.

Mollymawks are hoeing into the fish through the netting but luckily there's no seals around. Sea maggots. Des has no sympathy for seals: bite the tails off fish and left them. More wasteful and vicious than even fishermen, are seals. He's shot a few in his time. One or two fucking people could do with a shooting too. He unshackles the wing chains.

Bob's stopped the forward winch. He comes down to the stern, grapples the net with the lifting hook and winds the rope round the surge drum. The warp wires slacken as the big net-roller on the gantry takes over. The net begins to come aboard.

'That's the bunt,' Des calls to the kid, as he whacks tangled dogfish down towards the cod-end.

The floats bobble out of the sea and up to the net-roller like a giant's balls passing overhead. The floats are soon covered by winding layers of net. Water crashes out of the crushed net like a Niagara Falls.

'You've missed some,' calls the kid. He's pointing up to the net-roller where a dozen or so small flounder are being wound into the winch and bisected by mesh.

Bob, peppered with net water, glares at the kid with malevolent disbelief. 'Jesus, now he's a fucking Greenie.'

'Stickers,' Des calls back. 'Can't be helped.'

The cod-end comes up, hissing with water. It looks like a huge, pulsing heart with cut-off arteries made by the mouths of a thousand dismayed fish.

Talk is useless over the manic screams of the scrabbling gulls.

The cod-end swings aboard. Bob pulls the cod-end rope—the 'Jesus knot' some call it. The fish avalanche onto the deck. Not a bad catch: mostly flats, a good selection of rounds. A 25-pound conger eel bursts out of the maul and swims across the deck on its own slime.

You get the net back as fast as you can.

Des waits for Bob to retie the Jesus knot. No one touches that knot but the skipper. If it's left untied, or comes undone, there's no question of who's to blame. Captain goes down with his own slip.

The net peels off the roller and slithers back into the sea. Birds go crazy as the sun-fried stickers fall up to the surface and the avian fucking decibel level goes up a notch higher.

Ten minutes later they're trawling again.

The fish lie in a spreading heap, slowly skidding across a lava of desperate slime.

Unnatural. Species that never went near each other are lying cheek by jowl on the labouring deck. Just lying there, panting, writhing, squirting out that slime that is their only cure for contagious diseases like airlessness. Soon they'll be split —reduced to bony blueprints—and thrown away as frames.

Gurnard are grunting pathetic warnings, embolised puff-fish have blown up into spiky balloons in protection against a force they'd never dreamt of. They roll uselessly back and forth across the wallowing deck.

All these fish. These embers of fish. They just lie there, puffing, dying the politest deaths we know. Eyes wide in nightmare, every one of them right now seeing a ghost.

Royce

Holy shite! A skate hurls towards Royce, flapping its wings through the air like it does underwater. It crashes into a plastic box behind him, thrown by Des. Another, much bigger, is inexplicably thrown back over the side by Bob.

More skates fill the box. On top they are black, with intelligent, Oriental eyes. Underneath they are white with short square mouths and perfectly even fangs. Now and then an upside-down skate in the box mimes a cry of agony, arching upwards and somehow forming a huge perfect 0 with its square mouth.

Des and Bob are kneeling beside the pile, sorting the documents of fish into boxes. They wear aprons and rubber gloves and work with amazing rapidity. Big skates, little flounders and 'rubbish' fish are flung back into the sea. Most of all there seem to be flounders. Two cases with STOLEN FROM SCULLEYS stencilled on the side have been filled with them and Bob goes for more.

'Five types of flounder,' he says. 'That's an English flounder—very white underneath. That's a turbot, spots on the belly. That's a brill, yellow.'

'And that's a witch,' says Des, holding up a slightly smaller flounder, which didn't seem to have done anything to deserve the unkind name. 'It's got right-hand guts—all other flounders have left-hand guts. And it's full of little bones—impossible to eat.' He throws it over the side.

'When someone you don't like pesters you for flounders,' said Bob, 'you give them a sack of witches.'

Water from the net above them falls onto some of the fish, giving them a false lease of life. A new flapping frenzy breaks out, for about a minute. The last minute.

The last fish to die is a John Dory. It was the only one they've caught and for some reason it goes in the bin with the sharks. It stays alive long after there is silence in all the other bins. It stares up out of one sideways eye that has never seen the other, and makes little Mexican waves with its continuous fins.

On the way home he steers. You set the direction you want on the compass then look up and find a landmark behind it and you steer towards that. At first you're using clouds on the horizon or the smoke of the cement works until Westport comes up out of the sea and you use bits of landscape.

As they approach the tip head, Bob comes to stand on the bridge. 'I want 65,' he says. Royce hauls the boat this way and that until the compass points towards about 70. 'Sixty-five, I said!'

Compasses will not keep still and you're forever chasing them. 'Steer the boat, not the fucking compass!' roars Bob.

You start to get a feel for it, you realise that to steer to a direction you're always steering past it, going from one side of it to the other, so as soon as the boat is heading towards your compass point you start turning the wheel in the other direction, because you just know the fucking prow is gonna go right past it. In that zigzaggy way you aim yourself towards the bar.

'See those two red lights down the river? Steer at them.'

Royce never takes his eyes from them again. His sight aches. Every last gram of yesterday's stew is piling up at the backdoor of his sphincter. His mind reels with the memory of losses on the bar: overturnings, strandings, 4 killed in the sea off Westport every year . . .

'I can't do this, Bob,' he whimpers, 'you've got to take it in over the bar.'

'We crossed the bar 3 minutes ago, you fucking soft-cock,' growls Bob.

Royce looks round. On either side are the crude homely walls of the tip head. 'I drove across the fucking bar!' he laughs, and Bob laughs toothlessly beside him.

~ ~ ~

Big Shot

~

NORMAN MARSH

With other members of the fishing club I was watching the opening scenes of *Casting in the Sunset*, an American film promoting flylines and starring an angler who could have been recruited from the nearest rodeo. I can't recall his name, Bud or Hank, no matter, suffice to say he was resplendent in a cowboy hat, a smart fishing vest emblazoned with a dozen fishing club patches, razor-pressed trousers and highly polished boots. To be fair, he didn't wear spurs. The camera zoomed onto a brightly coloured packet and the tackle maker's name filled the screen.

'Is your system balanced?' followed by 'Are you getting the best out of your outfit? If not just watch an expert', capping it with, '*He* uses *Big Shot* flylines!'

After more of the sponsor's plug the commentator left it to Bud to deliver the goods. Standing, back to the camera, at the end of a long jetty he soon had the rod flexing in time to his jaws, inevitably chomping on gum. The line swished back and forth in long beautiful loops. With about a football pitch length out, another half spool followed and the fly must have landed somewhere on the horizon. He didn't quite pick his teeth at the same time but you could tell he could if he wanted to.

He soon had me sitting on the edge of my chair, I can tell you. Even if the nearest snag was half a mile away and he was standing in the middle of a lake, it was pretty impressive. It was when Buddyboy started to speak that I really took notice. In no uncertain terms I was informed that because I wasn't using the second layer of humbroid muscles, especially the ones nearest the spatula, I had spend the past 40 years or so doing it the wrong way. He made it quite clear that any Philistine with the elbow in and flexing the wrists could in no way expect to fish the celestial streams with Walton, Halford or Skues.

A sideways glance showed the intent faces of my fellow members, enthralled with this master caster. The youngest of them still had time to recover but for the likes of me, on the wrong side of 60, I was doomed to carry on catching trout using my firmly entrenched terrible casting habits. Perhaps if I had seen the film during my impressionable years, my trout catches would have doubled and I inwardly groaned, thinking of those wasted, especially designed, casting muscles.

Meanwhile, our angling cowboy, after now having performed with consummate skill the Rollcast, Speycast, Steeplecast, Forecast, Overcast and Downcast, proceeded to astound us with the Oregon Sidewinder, Spiral Uplifter and the famous Figure Eight Double Haul, the uplifter obviously created to skim the fly along the surface and jump over the odd low-lying willow branch while the double haul was meant for hard-to-reach trout lying on the other side of the Mississippi.

I think it was when he picked up *two* rods and sent a pair of orange torpedo heads into the sunset that I began to realise that under real battle conditions Bud might have lost a little of his poise. Perhaps, like me, with the line tangled around my ears and half a dozen wind knots in the leader, he could be muttering wild obscenities. For a start it wouldn't be on a 100-hectare lake on a windless day. There would be a 20-knot sou'wester shooting up his shorts, downstream of course, and a row of willows like picket fences on either bank. In addition, a droopy Taranaki fence over the stream to cast under and a bonfire-size pile of driftwood to cast over. Under those conditions I reckon it doesn't matter whether you've got the old elbow tucked in, or wagging like a dog's tail. It's getting the damned line out at all that matters, and if I'm lucky enough to fool the odd fish I'm very happy, and probably very lucky. Despite my ignorance of gumboil muscles or whatever is rippling away behind the scenes, my old line, miraculously, sometimes pops the fly smack onto the trout's dinner table.

Meanwhile, back at the ranch, and struggling to keep up with Bud's treatise on line weights, ball bearing surfaces, parabolic rod tapers, tensile strengths and ring friction, I wasn't disappointed when once again a zoom shot of the label appeared with a final reminder to buy Big Shot lines and join the 'who's who' of the angling world. On the way home with fellow members I felt more of a 'has been' than a 'who's who' but my spirits rose when Bill, from a back seat, summed the film up.

'Fishin's become more of a bloody science these days', he drawled.

And, looking back over the years when an old, but well cared for level line and an equally old slightly warped split cane rod amounted to a princely outfit, and trout thought none the worse of you for it, I had to agree.

~ ~ ~

Wet But Not Stumped

~

BOB SOUTH

They might have been exceptional as international cricketers, but the first thing to find out was if English batsmen Alan Lamb and John Morris could actually cast a fly line.

The Pommy pair had expressed an interest in catching an elusive New Zealand trout while in Wellington for the second of a one-day series against the Kiwis in the late 1980s. Lamb had told a *Herald* sportswriter Don Cameron, who later told me, that he desperately wanted to land a Taupo trout before the cricket tour ended.

At every stop in this country, Lamb had spun post-game, late-night yarns to all who would listen of his exploits catching salmon on the fly in England. Apparently, the likeable South African-born 35-year-old always ended these one-sided animated, conversations with tales of how his previous fishing attempts in New Zealand had always ended abortively without a rainbow or a salmon in the net, let alone in a fry pan.

Two discreetly placed phone calls later, raft company owner Garth and Turangi professional fishing guide Peter had graciously agreed to try to change Lamb's luck and that of 26-year-old team-mate Morris. So, two days before England lost by 7 runs to New Zealand in the decisive third one-dayer in Auckland, here we all were—Garth, Peter, Lamb, Morris, myself, close Taupo friend Pete D, and photographer Phil—at Begg's Pool putting in our two rafts to catch these guys a fish.

Two rapids down the Tongariro River and Peter ordered the Brits to exit the boat and trot their stuff with weighted nymphs. It quickly became apparent that both could cast and present a fly well enough to enjoy success. Both had early difficulties mastering the finesse of properly mending their lines, but for guys who had never nymph fished before they were extraordinary.

The runs below several of the grade 3 rapids further downstream beckoned now that Peter realised the day wouldn't be spent teaching total novices. Garth, an avid angler himself, steered his self-bailer proficiently through an especially technical section of white water, then pushed his boat into the bank. Soon, Peter waded Lamb to a likely pocket across the river, while Morris went downstream several hundred yards.

Using tiny Hare and Copper nymphs, Morris struck first, landing several fingerlings before picking up a nice 3-pound hen. Perched precariously on a midstream boulder, only yards above a rapid, Morris gingerly played the fish to his feet and was helped by Pete D to land it.

Seconds later, a yelp from upriver signalled that Peter had Lamb into the 6-pounder they'd spotted during the wade across. Rod bending fiercely, Lamb revelled in the challenge. He fought the fish for perhaps 10 minutes, while Peter waded back across to grab his net. Sadly, by the time Peter had navigated the navel-deep water, Lamb's trophy had broken off, taking the fly and a foot of trace with it. The pool now totally disrupted, a decision was made to move on.

The boat fair bubbled with excitement as it set off through several deep bits of likely holding water. The cricketers wondered aloud why they couldn't stop to have a flick at fish in one of the pools which scattered as the raft cruised over. But Garth and Peter, intent on reaching more productive pockets, pushed on.

Pulling onto a gravel bar smack in the middle of the river, again guides and anglers disembarked. A 3-pound kelt was rising under a small cliff face in the backwater and Peter wanted Lamb to test his skill. It would be a quick take, or nothing. This fish would probably spook after one or two casts. Carefully, Lamb plopped his fly several feet above the nose of the rainbow. Whack! The fish gobbled the invitation and Lamb broke his duck.

Through several tougher white-water rapids, Lamb and Morris warmed to the rafting experience, ever eager to get to the next fishing destination

Again, Garth, with the precision of a rally driver, rammed his boat between several rocks, deliberately locking it in place just at the apex of a fork in the river. Behind him, Pete D came up the backside of Garth's raft, secured it to Garth's with the bow rope, and everyone jumped out to peruse the water. Casually checking out another backwater on the true left bank, Peter and Lamb dismissed it as not worth fishing and decided to try the main flow on the true right. However, Pete D, after a more careful search, managed to spot a trout in the shallow that uncharacteristically escaped Peter's attention.

A few friendly jibes later—about who was the better fish spotter and who wasn't—and Lamb was into a 5½-pound fresh run rainbow. It was a superb fighting fish, making several good runs, before planting itself stubbornly in the deepest part of the current.

The battle was made all the more exciting when two boatloads of white-water rafters arrived unexpectedly, saw Lamb fishing, and turned what should have been a private occasion into a public one as they waited to see the superstar complete his mission. While Lamb tired the fish, several other trout were sent scrambling nervously round the pool. Once landed, Lamb's fish became the centre of photographic attention, leaving Morris to try his hand at hooking one of the remaining 4 still there.

An assortment of fly changes failed to do the trick for Morris, although Lamb, finally escaping modelling duties, returned to the main flow and ripped into a handful of fingerlings—'English fish' he called them—without enticing another large trout. All the activity had created an evil hunger among the raft-fish convoy. The most pleasant surprise of the afternoon was unveiled about halfway down the river where Garth had set up a virtual river-bank café.

A portable table, buried in the bow of one raft, was unrolled from its canvas sack and erected in the wet sand. Four chairs, pre-placed for just such an outing, mysteriously materialised from the beech trees lining the bank. A blue-chequered tablecloth was unfurled to adorn the table. Copious quantities of tucker and a bottle of white wine were rustled from the chilly bin. It was a meal fit for kings in an environment unfit for any other than the purist and keenest of freshwater anglers.

The late afternoon-early evening fishing proved less successful. Many fish were sighted, many undersized trout were caught, but only one real chance at a decent fish eventuated.

A deep pool eased into a shallow run at its tail. Up to 5 fish were sighted in the run, including one rising to naturals. Peter had Morris, the taller of the two shortish batsmen, wade the tailout to get to the opposite bank. He would attack, sort of from silly mid-on, from there. Lamb, conversely, stayed at the side of Garth and Peter, around mid-wicket, and had first crack with a dry. One fish did rise to the dry, nosed it gently but refused to be fooled. Morris had several casts to the group after that heart-pumping drama, had a take, but proved fractionally late on the strike.

As it so often does in timeless situations such as this special raft-fishing expedition, time had caught us up. The sun was slipping from view, hidden now by the fern-lined gorge walls of the Tongariro. It was approaching 7 pm and more than an hour's rafting remained to get home.

With all the charm of an adolescent desperate to continue a full-on, fun pursuit, Lamb asked—no begged—to have a few final casts. Time would not permit, he was told. Disappointment shown on his face as if he'd just been clean bowled on 99 with the last ball before stumps.

The experience wasn't finished, though. Unbeknown to Lamb and Morris, the best rapid of the Tongariro descent was still to come: the testing Whitikau

Hole, just above where the main spawning tributary, the Whitikau River, enters the Tongariro.

A large undetectable, submerged rock situated in the middle of the rapid creates a special turbulence and hydraulic effect that has a nasty habit of dumping clients, both white-water and raft-fishing ones, into the drink.

Garth opted to run the rapid the hard way, side-on, to maximise the thrill for his guests. His 14-foot boat came in sideways all right. Only trouble was, Morris was badly positioned to ride the fall. He resembled a rodeo cowboy riding a Brahman bull. As the boat bucked and buckled, Morris's only contact with it was a safety rope on the side. But for his grasp of the rope, he at one stage, completely airborne, had no other contact with the raft. Still he managed to hang on, although he came up drenched in the process, and made some fairly horrific faces in his time of panic. He survived only to hear Lamb laughing hysterically.

Something about raft-fishing the upper reaches of the Tongariro empties the mind of all worries, all stress, all pretence. It recharges the spirit, and produces unparalleled levity. Even for superstars.

~ ~ ~

The Lady Fishermen

~

ANNE FRENCH

Imagine Jane Austen in thigh waders perfecting
her rolling cast, or Miss Elizabeth Barrett
dashing off to the bush for a weekend's
pig-shooting. Mrs Melville perhaps, at the helm
for the two a.m. watch while Herman snatched
some sleep? Ludicrous. There's no tradition.
We'll just have to improvise (with improvements).

Take yesterday, for instance, drift fishing
in the dinghy off Rakino, five snapper in an hour.
Hauled up from thirty feet they screeched
as their swim bladders burst. Dead on arrival
in the bucket. And tonight I performed the graceful
act in my civilized kitchen: a sharp knife turning
one fish into two fillets and a pile of odds and ends.

Almost taken in by it, the poetry of catching
dinner, the magic of flesh turning white in the pan,
golden in its jacket of crumbs, decorated with a salad
of tomatoes and red onions as lurid as a paperback.
You might prescribe it as a known antidote to *branlement*
littéraire (that common affliction). Emily, pulling
steadily on the oars; Janet, slicing up the mullet bait.

~ ~ ~

Branlement: coined from the verb *se branler*—to wank.

Fishing — A Golfer's Perspective

~

GREG TURNER

I awoke with a start. That oh-shit-phone-where-am-I-what-time-is-it feeling rushed over me. 'Hello?'

'Auckland air traffic control here. We've been asked to inform you that Mr Faldo's flight arrived early so he'll be in Queenstown at 8.30 rather than 9.30,' an all too cheerful voice told me.

'Thanks,' I replied, trying not to sound too irritated. I looked at my bedside clock. It showed 6.15. Thanks, Nick, I thought as I rolled over and went back to sleep.

I don't know whether golfers or fishermen are worse when it comes to consideration toward others. Both probably like to think that their respective pastimes epitomise cultured behaviour. The fine arts of flinging a fly or swinging a club engender thoughts of gentlemanly conduct, of impeccable behaviour in a traditional sense. As with many such widely held but seldom contemplated assumptions the truth is probably some distance from perception. Both pursuits actually require a great degree of concentration, determination and persistence. Technique must be sound and nerve must be steely—no room for a moment's hesitation when either a pressure putt or a big feeding brownie presents itself. Quite often the requirements of both sports result in a single-minded selfishness that tends to run roughshod over the rights of others. On this particular morning I felt I had the right to a couple of hours' more shut-eye rather than a rushed trip to the airport. So I had it.

At 8.45 the phone rang again. 'Nick here, where are you?'

'I'm in bed of course—would have been up ages ago but some bastard called about 6 and woke me up. Took a while to get back to sleep after that. Still, I'm awake now so I'll be there soon. Grab yourself a cuppa.'

'Oh . . . all right . . . I'll see you soon.' The phone went dead and I chuckled at the thought of Nick grumpily heading into the terminal for a cup of tea. Those who fly around in chartered private aircraft aren't used to being treated with indifference.

I wandered downstairs to the kitchen where, true to form, Heggy (Swedish golfer and fly-fishing addict Joakim Haeggman) was already well into his third bowl of muesli and was surveying a newly acquired box of dry flies. Looking at the concoction that threatened to crawl out of his bowl, it occurred to me that one day he'd accidentally drop a Royal Wulff into his breakfast and end up with a pierced tongue. Best argument I'd yet thought of for barbless hooks.

To call Heggy intense when it comes to his twin loves would be akin to calling an Australian cricketer a bit brash. Heggy was proof that the archetypal Swedish sportsman was not necessarily a Bjorn Borg clone since he was as likely to explode on the first tee as the last. In rugby terms he'd be admired for being 'fired up' whereas in golf such a trait tends to be regarded as a weakness rather than a strength.

Nick, we figured, would by now be suffering from an ever-increasing case of lack of gruntle, so it was best we organised ourselves quickly. Into the back of the fishing wagon went the day's kit and we headed off. The forlorn Faldo flopped into the back seat, trying but failing miserably to hide his irritation, but after a short discussion on the day's schedule he cheered noticeably. The sky was clear, the temperature was rising and there was little sign of a breeze. Any annoyance at the delay was soon replaced with that infectious optimism that tends to befall fishermen early in the day when the weather is ideal.

We headed up the lake (Wakatipu) towards the sleepy hamlet of Glenorchy. A small airstrip fringes the road almost opposite the Greenstone Valley and this was where we were to be met by our helicopter (people who regularly charter aeroplanes don't bother to walk up valleys either).

I always feel less fulfilled by an excursion if the journey part is replaced by what is essentially a relocation process. There's something about a valley slowly unfolding before you, the anticipation that is enhanced by both the time and effort spent in hiking into a pristine environment. Mind you, although a short flight in may reduce this pleasure, the loss pales into insignificance by comparison with the deflation of watching someone else fly in just above the location to which you've just laboured.

We dropped in near the old homestead in the Caples Valley. The Caples is one of my favourite valleys although the fishing is only average. Stories abound of 'the good old days' before the road from Kinloch to the mouth of the Greenstone. The catch-22 of fishing the backcountry seems to be that the easier the access the more the fishing deteriorates, but having just choppered in it was difficult to feel aggrieved. The river is the ideal size—small enough to be able to be crossed with relative ease but large enough to hold some lovely fish. Nick's eyes glowed; Heggy began to fidget with excitement. I, having been responsible for the choice of venue, tried my best to talk things down.

'It's not what it used to be but there're still a few fish around. I just love it for the environment—figure a fish or two is a bonus.' Nick smiled politely. Heggy didn't even pretend to buy into it.

We assembled our rods, put on 3 different dries and headed to the river. Signs were good: in the first run we came to a nice-sized rainbow feeding away happily and apparently thankfully. Nick duly appointed himself first to tee off and, with his first cast, softly landed a Black Gnat a couple of metres upstream of his prey. Almost in slow motion the fish rose to the surface and—bingo!—a 2-kilogram rainbow was soon flapping on the shore. Heggy was by now in a state of near frenzy and, such was his enthusiasm to get to the next piece of holding water, he rushed straight past a 3-kilo brownie stationed at the top of the same run in which we'd hooked the rainbow. As it shot away downstream the realisation of what had just occurred washed over Heggy in a wave of annoyance. He dropped to his knees among the tussock and started pounding the ground. 'Relax,' I said, attempting to comfort. 'I'm sure there are plenty more where he came from.' Of course there weren't. The next 3 runs proved barren and Heggy looked concerned.

'If only I'd been a bit more careful,' Heggy lamented. If only—a phrase as often heard on the golf course as by the river.

We slowly moved upstream, perhaps being overly careful not to pass by another feeding fish, and had some success. By lunchtime Nick had landed two more healthy rainbows, Heggy had landed two and lost one and even I had managed a beautifully conditioned 3-kilogram brown. The mood among the party was jovial.

Just above the mid-Caples hut, the river runs through a small gorge at the top of which is an ideal place for lunch. There also happens to be a deep, fast-flowing pool that seems to be home to a monster brown. This particular fish has been interviewed on a regular basis but I have heard of no one catching him. I explained the situation to the boys, suggested we could sit on the bluff above, have lunch and watch him feed. I assured them that to try to catch him was pointless. The combination of the depth of water, the inaccessibility of the position needed to cast for him and his caginess meant that any attempt was a waste of time. Nick weighed up the situation and concurred. Heggy, on the other hand, was less prepared to accept my assessment.

'People don't catch him because they aren't determined enough,' he proclaimed.

'Heggy, that's not it. The only place you have a hope of catching him from is that gravel shelf in the middle of the river and the only way to get there is by coming down past him. He can't help but see you!' I explained.

'But you could climb down that cliff over there, drop into the river and ease your way up.'

'Heggy, you'd need to be Ed Hillary to get down that face and even if you did the water's 5 metres deep at the bottom.'

Heggy wasn't to be deterred. Nick looked at me, rolled his eyes and settled down to eat his sandwich while Heggy headed downstream. About 10 minutes passed until eventually he reappeared, this time in the river. He was picking his way along the side of the chasm, one hand grasping at hand-holds, the other extended vertically out of the water holding the rod, and his feet kicking hard. It looked a bit like a cross between synchronised swimming and a training course for the Marines. When he reached the point just opposite the gravel shelf, he pushed off quietly and in a sort of one-armed dog paddle eased across the river.

Now, if you've ever been in one of those snow-fed rivers and had the water get much above knee height you'll know just how cold it can be. The thought of it being up to your neck—holy hell! Safely at his shelf, Heggy began to drag himself on his belly. Soaking wet and covered in fine silty gravel, he was quite a sight. When he reached the end of the shelf he was still a good 10 metres downstream of the leviathan. Still on his belly, he let the fly fall softly onto the water and, slowly stripping line, used the current to take out the necessary length. His quarry was meanwhile merrily feeding away about a metre deep but every so often his snout would break the water as he fed on something in the surface film. By now Heggy had quietly dragged himself onto his knees. The time was right; he lifted the rod tip just high enough to make a cast. Before the fly had even passed him on the way upstream our fishy friend had sunk to the bottom of the chute—some 5 metres down.

'Where'd he go?' yelled Heggy.

'He's still there. He's just doing an impersonation of a submarine. You might as well forget him. Hell of an attempt though.'

No such luck. Heggy wasn't about to give up that easily. He fished around in his nymph box and produced the biggest weighted Hare and Copper he could find. Realising he'd be there for some time, I suggested to Nick we'd better head on. 'He'll get sick of it sooner or later and catch up.'

We covered quite a bit of territory before we found another trout, and this one was feeding in a very awkward position, just downstream of an overhanging branch. To get the required drift would mean a very flat cast, almost horizontal to the ground, so the fly would reach a point under the overhang. Nick set about the task, firstly heading about 10 metres down the river to practise the required technique.

As I watched him, it occurred to me how similar golf and fishing really were. Nick's temperament when performing in either pursuit was essentially the same. Intense concentration, meticulous preparation and a zest for technical excellence were every bit as apparent on the river as the golf course. When you're fishing there are multiple considerations to take into account. After you've located the trout.(no mean feat in itself) then comes the process of determining what it's feeding on, what depth of water it's in and where you need to land the fly in order to present it to the fish in a natural manner. Then comes the dilemma of where to position yourself, given wind conditions and backcast obstacles, and how to do so without being detected. Only once all of that is sorted out must you deal with the technical requirements of making the cast needed and the mental process of producing the right cast at the right time. Any weakness in this chain of events is likely to result in the fishing equivalent of a double bogey.

In golf there exists a very similar scenario. You have to determine a strategy to play a hole based on the obstacles present, the wind direction and velocity and the pin placement on the green. You then go about performing the technical necessities of the golf swing to produce the desired result. More often than not you will be required to adapt your plan along the way and therefore have to solve a number of both technical and cerebral problems. In the end, as often as not, it will be the ability to focus your attention and then produce the optimum per-formance at the most important juncture that will determine whether the outcome will be successful.

And precise you must be for, in a world increasingly infected with a disease called sycophancy, the trout and the golf ball are, even if inadvertently, both equally contemptuous of reputation, fame or celebrity. Through the eyes of a fish or the dimples of a golf ball we are all truly equal.

As I watched him preparing to face this very difficult challenge, the Nick Faldo I saw on the river was the same as the one I was all too familiar with on the golf course. Same mannerisms, same concentration, same determination, same focus. Same result too, for when it came time to produce this most difficult cast he did so with unerring efficiency. The fish spotted the little dry, poked its snout quietly out of the water and was just about to sip it in when out of the bush stumbled Heggy. With a swish of its tail, the fish darted in under a matagouri-clad overhang and sank to the bottom. If looks could kill, Heggy would have been horizontal on the river bank in a pool of blood. As it was, he looked like something out of a Michael Jackson video, with bits of mud and gravel attached to just about every inch of his body. He had finally succumbed to the monster of the gorge and, in his hurry to catch up with us, had walked in at precisely the wrong moment. Nick was fuming, I was trying not to show my amusement and Heggy was just looking sheepish.

Again, as with golf, wallowing in either frustration or annoyance serves little purpose. There was plenty more river to explore, more fish to interview and more mistakes to be made. But in the end it all matters little if you make one perfect cast at the right moment and have the reward of a fish rising to your enticement.

The day moved into evening, more and more of the river became enveloped in shadow and the fish were less apparent. All too soon our oversized bumblebee arrived to whisk us back to what we call civilisation. And as we sat around the barbecue that evening, sipping wine and reliving every cast, it occurred to me that we had never once spoken of golf. Three golfers together for an entire day and no mention of flying right elbows or explosive hip turns. It was bliss—the game never thought of yet many valuable lessons learnt. For a day on the river is far more rewarding than any day spent on the practice range.

~ ~ ~

The Fabulous 'Flattie'

~

NOEL BATY

The modest, retiring flatfish. Surely one of the epicurian treats from the bountiful waters of our country, available to almost any who care to take the time and make the effort to secure them.

The variety is fairly wide: we have 4 species in New Zealand, excluding the larger brill and turbot which grow to a very large size, and are resident mainly in the South Island. Turbot are the fattest of the flat fishes, and are found mainly between Dunedin and Bluff. On occasions they have been deep-trawled as far north as Whangarei, but these occurrences are rare. Turbot are brownish to reddish in colour, and one of the largest recorded was 762 millimetres in length.

Brill are more common, and according to records grow larger than turbot. The largest recorded brill is a shadow under a metre in length and weighed 6.8 kilogram. Mention is made of these two species purely as a matter of interest, because the chances of you running your spear through one, or finding one in your net, are remote, to say the least.

The most common 'flattie' is the sand flounder (pakiti). He's found over the length and breadth of New Zealand, in tidal creeks, rivers and estuaries. In some instances flounder have been found many kilometres up quite small creeks, as far as the brackish water extends. Baby flounder start life as small round-bodied fish but a strange metamorphosis occurs during the first few weeks of life. The left eye begins a slow movement across the little flounder's head until it joins the right eye. During this transformation the mouth becomes distorted and the body begins to flatten. The small fish now drifts to the sea bed where it completes the change to a fully formed but immature flatfish.

You could regard the flatfish as being the opposite end of the scale when thinking of the distribution of the ocean's fishes. The pelagic (surface feeding) tunas, kahawai, kingfish and many others occupy the top stratum, snapper and many other species range between the bottom and mid-water, then the flatfish occupy the lowliest (as well as lowest) position of all. Nature has provided the oceans with feed organisms throughout its depths, and the various species of fish have adapted to share the feed chain. The same applies to land mammals: the carnivores, herbivores and the omnivorous species ensure that all have access to sustenance. Were it otherwise the food would go to the strongest and all others would perish.

Flatfish live solely (pardon the pun) on tiny crustacea and other minute organisms. As they grow, small crabs and other slightly larger particles come their way and are gladly accepted. The fisherman's wiggly worm or a succulent slice of pipi or mussel will be taken eagerly, and this form of fishing for flounder is highly entertaining and profitable.

My own first attempts at rod fishing for flounder were made with a little threadline rod and Ambidex threadline reel. A couple of split shot were pinched on the line about a foot or so above the two hooks which were baited with whole worms. At low tide the worms were tossed over the lip of the shallow water and as the tide advanced the flounders came with it. This is not always the case, of course—there's nothing certain about fishing with line. There are times of feeding activity and times of quiet. Times of movement, times of stillness. Naturally the times of feeding and movement are likely to be the most productive, if you're using a line and bait. Before launching forth into details of rigs and methods, let's take a look at the other types of flattie we're likely to find.

The New Zealand yellow-belly (patiki-totara) has a dark grey upper surface and even darker marking on the fins. The underside (right side) is yellow with sundry dark splodges—the obvious yellow underside is the reason for the popular name. Yellow-belly are widely distributed throughout the country and can be found in or close to river mouths. These flounders dine early on small crabs, shrimps, marine worms and brittle stars as well as immature shellfish of different species. Garden worms are also readily accepted so in addition to small slices of pipi, bits of mussel or seaworm the yellow-belly's diet is quite widely varied.

The green-back is thought by many to be the most succulent of the flatfish (excluding brill which I've found to be the finest). The belly of this flounder is pure white, and the fish itself has a markedly pointed nose. This flounder has a very small mouth, and size 14 trout hooks rigged double in tandem are necessary, otherwise the fish tends to nibble the worm up to the hook and reject what's left. I've not seen any green-backs in the north, but when I lived in Canterbury we came across them in estuaries and harbours.

The black or river flounder (patiki-mohoao) rather resembles the sole in shape, and in fact could be confused with a sole by hasty identification. While the species discussed previously have rather pointed snouts, the black has a rounded snout; not as rounded as the sole, but nearly so. Also, it is not actually black, but a very dark green, spattered with red spots.

There are two species of sole in our water, the common sole ('poor soul') or (patiki-rori) and the lemon sole. I've speared many common sole in local rivers near the mouths, and find them little different in flavour to the flounder. Maybe I was unlucky, but one night's catch of sole was unpalatable due to a strong muddy flavour that I had not encountered before or since. They grow to a greater size than flounders, one specimen recorded being 686 millimetres in length. The average is nearer to 450 millimetres.

Sole tend to move into shallow water in the hotter weather, but soon seek deep water when the seas come up rough. The common sole is greenish-grey above, and white below. Its food is wide ranging and includes juvenile fish such as young pilchards and yellow-eye mullet.

The lemon sole dines on quite large forms of marine life, among which are small cod, 'bullies', and the offspring of any other species that happens to be in the immediate vicinity at tucker-time. The upper surface is coloured brown and grey, the underside a creamy colour.

Probably because of the high mortality risk of the free-floating ova, flounders and soles produce prodigious numbers of eggs. A million eggs in a ripe female flounder is about the norm, and drifting at the mercy of the tide and wind they become easy prey to pelagic feeders. Soles appear to obtain much of their food by probing the silty bottom with a small nipple-like protrusion on the lower jaw. Other food comes to them as they lie buried in the sand or silt, with just their eyes protruding.

Flounders and soles can be observed as they enter shallow water, sinking to the bottom and, with a few sharp wriggles, covering themselves almost completely. Often the outline of the fish can be seen, as well as the eyes. I remember one night while we were spearing at the mouth of the Awakino River, I noticed what looked like the outline of an enormous sole. Without much conviction I gave it a tentative prod with my spear, and away went the biggest flatfish I've ever seen. It would have fed the 4 of us!

We won't discuss nets or spears, as I suspect that spearing and netting, while constituting a pastime, do not come into the sport category of fishing. No doubt there will be some who will dispute this: good luck to them.

The greatest sport can be had by fishing for flatties with a light rod, fine nylon, tiny hooks and live worms. I have said my early efforts were with a thread-line rod and reel, well, the rod (rest my soul) was a Hardy Wanless splitcane. Had Mr Wanless known that his beloved brainchild, designed for the finest and most delicate angling that British trout streams could produce, was to be used for dunking a worm in salt water in pursuit of a flounder, then that gentleman might well have rotated rapidly in his grave. Nevertheless, the Wanless plus the Ambidex reel, with 2.5-kilogram line and a couple of No. 10 hooks served me well.

The first flounder I caught by this method was about 100 metres up a small tidal creek. We'd seen several snuggling their way along the flats early in the rising tide, so we found some worms and set to work to catch them. My rig was as mentioned, with a whole red worm on each hook. These were cast out to where the channel shelved up to the shallow, and were left to do their duty as flounder lurers. Sure enough, half a metre away, just over the lip, a big puff of mud clouded the clear water. Then a bit closer. A flounder was stalking the baits.

A couple more puffs, and we could clearly see him, a nice little fish about 300 millimetres in length. Trouble was, he came within taking distance of the lower worm, but wouldn't take it. I gave the line a bit of a twitch, moving it towards the shore. The flounder made no attempt to take so I commenced edging the bait towards the beach, and right on the line where the water and beach met, he grabbed. What a shemozzle! He bucked and bent, then, getting his head facing deep water, he took off like a trout with violent undulations of his body.

When I did manage to get him coming he fought strongly with powerful convolutions until I had him flapping madly on the beach. I tell you, my heart was beating as much as if I'd just landed a good trout. And I'm sure Mr Wanless would have beamed his approval, too.

～ ～ ～

Poetry Reading

~

RANGI FAITH

About the time
the first poet
took the floor,
a three and a half pounder
took my Mrs Simpson and fled,
the reel screaming;

the Arnold turned
into a leaden sheet
as the rain came in
over bush electric
with cicadas;

and when the light was beached,
shadows rode in
on the scent of the night
hunting;

therefore a toast to you
my friends,
and for your fishing,
kia ora.

~ ~ ~

A Fisherman's Winter Tale

~

NEVILLE BENNETT

Winter brings for anglers a season of contrary moods and indulgences. When the frost sets in, and summer becomes an ethereal memory, the angler may escape into reverie by desultorily checking his tackle. The rod bag is opened, one and then another joint is extracted. There is no intention to set the rod up, but setting-up inevitably follows.

The rod feels familiar and reassuring, yet a little unsatisfactory without the reel. The reel is added, and soon the angler wishes ceilings were higher. Are more rods smashed by architects' stinginess than plunging trout? Is that why Edward Gibbon, somewhere in *The Decline and Fall of the Roman Empire*, said architects are the enemy of mankind?

Unless the angler is very strong-minded, he begins to compare the first rod with a second (I ignore those grudging or tyrannised anglers who claim one rod is enough). Sometimes an extraordinary thing happens: the 'spare rod', which had been relegated in favour of a newer rod, reasserts its old influence. Old rods are sometimes like a laid-down wine: they emerge from obscurity with new characteristics.

However, matters might be less ideal and take an expensive turn. Sometimes the angler has an attack of equipment fetishism and looks upon his rods with an irascible frown. His favourite wand fails to cast far enough. Many missed opportunities can be explained by its patent shortcomings.

The reverie is over. Intolerance mounts. The rod becomes a poor, inadequate thing. The angler wonders how he contrived any success with such an unsuitable instrument. No wonder some friends have wiped his eye. Perhaps the angler owes it to himself to look around.

Thus the angler takes the irrevocable step towards adding to his collection. 'Accidentally' he finds himself in a shop; and he may as well have a look at the stock, since mere chance has directed his feet in that direction.

Chances are that two miracles will coincide. First, there will be a rod in the shop which seems hand-made for the angler. Secondly, it will be such a never-to-be-repeated-bargain-price that it would be extraordinarily silly to fail to grasp the opportunity. The imagination soars. Fish that escaped months ago would be easily conquered with this new aid.

These are genuine sentiments, for a new Penn 'Graphite Gold' lies on my desk. I had to share my good fortune with a friend. He rushed out and bought one too. We reckon the retailer must be feeling as sick as a parrot to have undersold himself twice!

Although the rod is mine, it isn't really owned until it has caught a fish. Come October, I'll escape from family and work obligations, and go fishing. After all, first things come first. I have a primary duty to fulfil the rod's destiny by catching a fish. Meanwhile, I'm almost sure I can make do with my old reel for another season.

～ ～ ～

The Angler

~

GRAEME LAY

People in the town said that Frank Watson knew more about fishing than anyone else in Kaimara. And duck shooting and deer stalking. During the week he ran the shop that supplied equipment and advice to the town's sportsmen, and at the weekends he practised what he preached.

Watson's Sportsgoods was a small shop between Peat's Drapery ('Clothes for the Fashion Conscious') and Hughsons' Books ('Take Us As Read'). But Watson's Sportsgoods had an allure that its neighbours could never match. How could holeproof socks, or the *Weekly News*, compete for interest with burnished cane rods, reels of stainless steel and unstrung tennis rackets whose open frames held the promise of a love match? Then there were the accessories: fishing lures of a hundred variegated hues, Judas bird decoy ducks, closed boxes of deadly ammunition, open boxes of fluffy white tennis balls and dimpled golf balls, and rugby balls whose virgin amber leather demanded booting.

And on the wall above the counter, mounted on polished oak boards, were the great trout that Frank Watson had taken from local rivers and lakes over the years, their eyes bulging, mouths fixed in a rictus of indignation. In pride of place, hanging a little higher than the others, was the 14-pound rainbow trout that Frank had enticed from Lake Taupo in August, 1967.

Frank was in his 60s and a widower. He was short and barrel chested, with grizzled hair cut very short, beady seagull eyes and a jutting lower jaw. He knew every pool and rapid in the river that looped through Kaimara's hinterland, and every bush-clad glen in the Ruakahu Range. He could weave a blind from raupo reeds and bring down a mallard in a May dawn drizzle. No life membership of the Acclimatisation Society had been harder earned or was more deserving than Frank Watson's. For over 30 years he had been willing to share his sporting knowledge with the town's sportsmen, young and old.

One afternoon in late September, 4 days before the new trout fishing season, two customers came into Watson's Sportsgoods. They were both 10 years old and both wore jeans, jerseys and gumboots. One had spiky blond hair and freckles and was a head taller than the other, who was slightly built, with black hair.

'Hello, boys. What can I do for you?' said Frank in his nasal voice.

The smaller boy spoke for both of them. 'Two trout licences, please.'

'Right you are.' He reached into a drawer behind the counter. 'All ready for Friday? Tackle in good shape?'

Both boys nodded eagerly, then gazed around at the rods, lures and landing nets, up at the mounted trout, plump and petrified, and down at the counter. Beneath the glass top, arrayed in trays on a black velvet background, were Frank Watson's hand-tied trout flies. Dozens of them, in colours of every hue, feathery wisps like exotic elfin brooches.

Watching the boys' eyes as they studied his creations, Frank took their money for the licences, then filled in the forms, stamped them and handed them over.

'There we are, all set for the new season. Going to use flies or bait?'

'Bait,' said the fair-haired boy. 'We're going up to the railway bridge after school to get some creepers.'

Frank stared at them over the top of his glasses. 'Mmm. Well, creepers aren't bad. But you won't get a rainbow trout with live bait. Or a really big brown, either. Too cunning.' He reached under the counter. 'This is what I'll be using on Friday morning.'

He held out the tiny fly, turning it over with his stubby fingers. The shaft was bound in black, striped with thin strips of gold thread, the feathered wings crimson, tipped with blue. The tip of the hook was just visible. The boys stared at the beautiful object, their mouths half open, looking themselves a little like fish about to strike.

'What's it called?' asked the smaller of the boys.

'Spring Rise. Made it myself.' He turned and looked up at the biggest of the mounted fish on the wall behind him. 'Got him with that one.' Looking back at the boys again, he said, 'Sure you wouldn't like to try using flies on Friday?'

The boys looked at each other for a moment, then the dark-haired one replied. 'No thanks, Mr Watson, we'll use creepers.' They both knew, and the old man did too, that with live creeper for bait they stood at least a chance of catching something on opening day, even if it was a brown just over the minimum size. Fly fishing was too slow. Frank gave a little chuckle.

'All right then. Good luck for Friday. I might see you somewhere along the river. If I don't, drop in and let me know how you got on. And don't forget'—he chuckled again—'the limit's 6 fish each!'

'Thanks Mr Watson,' each of them said in turn. 'Bye.'

It had been an unusually dry winter, and the river wound its way sluggishly through the paddocks. Along its banks worn stones were exposed, and dry weed and sticks crunched beneath their gumboots as they trudged along the edges of the riverbed. Only where the river narrowed, or fell, did the water tumble and break into whiteness, and where stretches of lupin drooped over the deeper sections its water lay as dark and shiny as a pool of oil. As they came to one of the pools the fair-haired boy stopped and pointed. 'Look!' A ring of ripples marked the spot where the trout had risen. As they stared they saw the sinuous shadow first glide, then dart downstream. 'Wow! Must have been at least a 5-pounder!'

'Yeah, at least. Wish Friday would hurry up.'

'Me too. Come on . . .'

They stumbled on, pausing only to watch a trout rise or to skim flat worn stones across the pools to the other bank. Under the railway bridge the gritty sand was cool and damp, and the sand beneath the stones yielded a good supply of writhing creepers. In 20 minutes they had a tobacco tin full of the larvae, and they moved off towards the track which led across the paddocks and back to the town.

But before they reached the track they were diverted by an urge to sit on top of the old dam which blocked the river a little way below the bridge. The dam had been built many years before, to impound the river water and channel it off so that electricity could be generated from its flow. The brainchild of an ambitious county engineer, the scheme was a costly folly which had soon fallen into disuse. The dam's internal machinery became clogged with silt, the diversion race overgrown with weed.

The boys knew none of this. They only knew that from the top of the concrete dam the view of the deep pool at its foot, the dry, bouldered watercourse below, and the paddocks and pine plantations beyond, was satisfying. They perched on the top of the dam, the water lapping only inches behind them, their legs dangling above the long concrete slope below. The only sound was the trickle of the overflow in the channel on the far side. The series of hollow concrete steps on the other side, included by the engineer to allow migrating trout to by-pass and ascend the dam, were filled with stones, the water within the steps shallow and stagnant.

The smaller boy looked more intently at the pool below the dam. He pointed. 'Look! Down there!'

'What? Oh . . . yeah . . .'

From high above, the shapes were visible. Trout. Dozens of them. Small trout. Large trout. Very large trout. Swimming casually, rising lazily in their own private pool. The boys continued to stare in silent disbelief.

'They must've got trapped there after a flood,' said the fair boy at last. 'Couldn't get up or down. Come on, let's go down and have a look . . .'

They stood on the concrete apron at the foot of the dam and gazed down into the pool. The trapped trout swam round and round, gliding, then darting into the shadows by the bank. The smaller boy took a creeper from the tin and tossed it into the water. The pool boiled and the insect vanished. The other boy picked up a handful of creeper and threw them in, closer to the edge. The trout fed, greedily, unafraid, and the boys were entranced.

'They're like those tame trout at Rotorua . . .'

'Yeah. Look at that one! Huge! Wish we had a line . . .'

'Couldn't. Have to wait till Friday. When the season starts.'

'Mmm. Let's get some more creepers, feed them up and get them used to us.'

'Okay. Then on Friday . . . But we'll have to keep it a secret. No telling anyone, not even Mr Watson.'

'No. No one. Until Friday.'

They sat at the foot of the dam, their rods put to one side. Between them were 12 brown trout. The dark-haired boy ran his forefinger along the speckled side of one of the fish and its gills quivered. Two of the others were still opening and closing their mouths, gulping in slow motion, but the eyes of all the fish were turning cloudy. The boys rearranged their catch yet again, this time in ascending order of size, then sat back and gazed at the haul. The chill of the early morning had gone, and the first day of October promised to be mild with only a slight breeze.

'Your biggest and my biggest are about the same size.'

'No, mine's bigger, look.'

'You bugger, that's mine.'

'No it's not!'

'It is!'

The small one grabbed the bigger one by the jersey and they had a pretend fight.

Then, panting, they stopped to admire the fish again, and agreed to weigh the two biggest when they got home.

'They'll both be over 4 pounds I reckon.'

'Yeah, bet they are. And I reckon we must've set a record.'

'What d'you mean?'

'Well, 12 trout in 20 minutes.'

'Hey yeah. And what about when the big one took your bait, then mine. Together.'

'Yeah, we'll have to call that one a draw. Hey, I know, let's take them up to Mr Watson's place and show him. There's time before school starts.'

'Okay. He'll be really chuffed that we *both* caught the limit on the opening day. Come on, let's get them all into the bag.'

Frank Watson lived in a small, cream-painted weatherboard house with a red corrugated iron roof, tucked away inside a privet hedge in a back street of the town. The boys pushed excitedly through the front gate and knocked at the front door. When he saw who it was, the old man smiled.

'Morning boys. How did it go?'

Their words tumbled out as each tried to outdo the other.

'Great Mr Watson . . .'

'We found this pool . . .'

'*Full* of trout . . .'

'They couldn't get out . . .'

'They were nearly tame . . .'

'We only had to drop in our lines . . .'

'And they took the creeper straight away . . .'

'And we got *12!*'

'In 20 minutes!'

'Look!'

They tipped the contents of the bag out onto the lawn by the front step in a slippery heap. The old man looked down at the pile of trout for a few moments, then at the two eager faces. He sucked at the inside of his mouth for a moment, then said, 'Wait there a moment, boys, I want to show you something too.'

When he reappeared he was holding a trout. A fair-sized rainbow, about a 2-pounder. Hooking a finger into its gills, he leaned against the door jamb and told them of his morning.

'I started at 5 o'clock, just above the rapids by the cattle crossing, using a Golden Gnat, a fly I made years ago. Had no luck there, so I walked upstream about half a mile and fished the pool under the willow trees, you know the one. I got onto a good one, a brown I think he was, and played him downstream. He was cunning though—got into white water and threw the hook. So I changed to a Spring Rise fly and tried that bend where the river runs below the cliff. It needed a long cast—there are those boulders in mid-stream and it's easy to get snagged—but after about 20 minutes I hooked this one.' He held the fish up. The colours on its flanks were not quite dull. 'The boulders gave him a 50-50 chance, and he put up a damn good fight.' Eyes still on the fish, he went on. 'That was all the luck I had today.' He pushed out his bottom jaw and looked at them hard over the top of his glasses. 'But he's what trout fishing's all about, boys.'

It was later that day, after school, when they came into his shop again. On the counter were pieces of the reel that Frank Watson was servicing. He looked up.

'Hello again, boys. What can I do for you?'

They looked at each other, down at the floor, then up at the mounted trout on the wall. Then the smaller one looked at him and spoke.

'We'd like to buy some trout flies please, Mr Watson.'

～ ～ ～

Pool

~

KEVIN IRELAND

In the snagged hollows of a river,
or the sockets between the willows
of a green creek, or sometimes below
the smudges at the edge of a lake

where the shingle spills into pits
of reeds—in lost labyrinths
of rock and root, King Trout
shoulders the dark and takes

the slow weight of the water.
Yet sometimes, on days of gladness,
when the last glimpse of setting sun
beads the water in a soft haze,

the old fish will jet from the deep
and splash graffiti across its ceiling
of air. The bold silver loops
of its scrawl catch at the edges

of sight, and in that instant you know
you saw more than just the flash
of its arc. King Trout turned
the world inside out. As he flew

through the sky you suddenly knew
both the bruise of that river (the crush
of that lake) and a wild rush of freedom,
the madness of breaking the rules.

~ ~ ~

A Day on the Mataura with Nancy Watson

~

BRIAN TURNER

When Nancy Watson rang and asked if I'd like to go fishing with her I jumped at the chance. 'Oath,' I said, 'any time you like.'

'Oh good, I was hoping you could come. Meet me at the station tomorrow morning, 9 o'clock. And bring your sleeping bag. We'll probably stay the night.'

I put the phone down and made a cup of coffee, to settle my nerves. Then I rang my mate Bill Kotzwinkle. 'Guess what,' I said, casually, coolly, 'Nancy's asked me to go fishing with her for a couple of days.'

Bill snorted. 'Not surprised. I'd heard Ricky Forster was away for a while and she was looking for someone. She's already asked Miguel Wendle, Alain McMillan, Pedro Barberossi, and Eduardo Ross. Me too, of course, but we all have to work.'

'Liar, Kotzwinkle, you're nothing but a born liar.'

'Indeed, a born angler.'

I was at the station by 8.30. Nancy arrived in her Toyota 4 x 4 on the dot of 9. Her honey-coloured hair was tied in a pony-tail and her stone-washed jeans were tight.

'Throw your gear in the back and jump in, brother.'

Nancy squirted through the intersection on the amber light and swung into a park opposite the tackle shop. 'I'll just slip in and pick up the hut keys from Sandy Maltman. Thought we'd stay at Riversdale. Horace Windley says the Mataura's been fishing well, especially in the evenings.'

Horace lives in spaced-out Waitati in a scruffy little welfare-funded 6-bedroomed shack complete with video, TV, compact disc player, drier, dishwasher, deep freeze, automatic washer and microwave oven. Horace's heroes are Roger Douglas and Richard Prebble; he admires them for remaining in Auckland. He also greatly admires Geoffrey Palmer for showing the world that Easter Island statues not only travel well but, provided they get the right sort of schooling, can actually learn to speak good English.

I often visit Horace in the evenings. Me and a few others, anglers and opera lovers. We lie about on the shag-pile drinking wine, eating oysters, mussels, cockles and crays, and listen to the glorious sounds of Pavlovarotti and our lovely little Kiri.

Sometimes Nancy Watson turns up with that tanned fit creep Ricky Forster who always brings his own supply of Carlsberg and refuses to drink anything else. Ricky even takes Carlsberg with him on fishing trips, the snoot, while we are happy, Horace and I—more than happy—to stick with Speights, the Pride of the South.

The weather improved the further we drove south and as we cruised over the downland west of Balclutha, autumn sunshine played on the paddocks of the impoverished.

Nancy said the day was warming up nicely. She said we should do all right. She said if Horace could catch fish in the Mataura anyone could. She said his casting was worse than mine, worse even than Wendle's, and certainly worse than Barberossi's.

'If this weather keeps up,' she said, 'we should catch heaps.'

Nancy has an impressive collection of tapes, including some early albums from the Hokey Pokeys, the Tail End Charlies, the Sexy Susannas, and the Droll Pongolians. She is also very fond of Van Morrison, especially classic albums such as *Astral Weeks* and *Moondance*. These, she says, are the 'essential Van'; she is not so keen on recent 'rather schmaltzy albums like *Avalon Sunset*'.

She is also quite a fan of Buster Poindexter's. Odd woman is Nancy Watson.

The gross and glossy plastic brown trout statue was glinting repulsively as we drove through Gore, the brown trout capital of the world. That is what Gore claims for itself, and yet, as Nancy sneeringly pointed out, 'the drips of councillors have just spent about 100,000 dollars of ratepayers' money on legal fees for opposing an application for a conservation order on the river'.

We decided to have a look at the water a few kilometres above the town. We had just finished tackling up and were about to head upstream when I spotted a little 4-wheel drive Suzuki whizzing across the paddock towards us. It pulled up alongside and out struggled old Freddie Baveystock.

'Freddie,' I said, 'this is Nancy. Nancy Watson.'

Freddie shook her hand and eyed her up and down, and up, and down. 'I think we've met before. At the Wyndham Anglers' Christmas party. You had an argument with Valerie Cooke.'

Nancy smiled. 'I'd forgotten her name. Valerie, that fits.'

Freddie asked us to wait, said he'd like to come with us, said he'd show us a backwater with at least 6 fish in it.'Tried to catch one of them yesterday. Not a chance. Tried them with Corixa, Black and Peacock, Hare's Ear, Midge, Willow Grub, Caddis . . . ignored the lot. Love to see that wonder boy Wendle have a crack at them.'

As we strolled towards the river Freddie hung back a bit and whispered to me,'They say she's pretty good. They say she's damned near as good as Wendle.'

'Better looking, that's for sure.'

Nancy had gone ahead, leaving me to follow more slowly with the tottery Freddie.

We came to a nasty-looking barbed-wire fence. 'Watch out,' said Freddie, giving me a wink,'you wouldn't want to rip the scrotal sack, eh.'And he cackled. 'Not with Ricky Forster being away.'

I rolled my eyes.'You're a dreamer, Freddie, a dreamer.'

Nancy had abandoned the stone-washed jeans for a pair of dark green shorts and was up to her gleaming brown thighs in a ripple when we arrived at the river. Her rod was bent and springing.

'God, she's got one on already.'Freddie was both envious and impressed.

Nancy toed the fish ashore, stooped, flicked the hook from its mouth and slipped the trout back into the river.

'Not worth keeping,'she said.

Freddie was aghast.'But that was nearly 3 pounds.'

'It was ripe. When I catch a nice fat little fish—one that's not going to spawn —I'll let you have it, Freddie.'And Nancy returned to the ripple.

Half an hour later we came to Freddie's fertile backwater. The fish were there all right. Eight of them, patrolling up and down.

Freddie cast and spooked the nearest fish. The second ignored his offerings. I too tried and failed. Unusual, that. Then Nancy tied on a large green fly with broad wings and a long tail which descended like a skydiver and quivered ever so slightly as it lay on the water. The biggest fish in the family just beat the others to it. Gulp. Nancy set the hook. The fish smashed the water to smithereens, rushed around the backwater 3 times, then streaked out into the main river.

Nancy leapt from the bank, struggled through deep mud and stumbled up a shingle bank, her rod bucking.'At last,'she said,'a real fish.'

Freddie was shaking.'Holy shit!'He shook his head.'She'll never land that.'

I smiled.

Nancy waded across the river, the water up to her waist, her rod high above her head.

I shuddered with admiration and thought what a marvellous standard bearer she'd make for the New Zealand team at the Barcelona Olympics.

It took her a quarter of an hour to subdue that fish and wrestle it ashore.

'How big is it?'

'At least 4 kilograms.'

Freddie was astounded. 'That's almost 10 pounds,' he said to me. 'Jesus, I'd love to flop that in front of old Ralph Bainbridge.' His voice was shrill when he sang out to Nancy: 'Keep it! Keep it!'

Nancy considered this. I rested my arm on Freddie's shoulder, just in case the poor little bastard was doomed to yet more disappointment. 'All right, Freddie.' Nancy banged the big fish on the bonce and waded back to us. 'Here,' she said.

Freddie clutched the fish in both hands and stowed it in his bag. Then he said, 'Thanks, but I'm off to the bowling club. Can't wait to show this beauty to old Ralph.'

Nancy caught 8 fish to my 2, the usual bath. But I didn't care. Some of us thrive on humiliation.

Later, in the hut, after a huge meal of broccoli, cheese, carrots, potatoes and rib-eye steak, plus hot cross buns and coffee, I said to Nancy, 'Tell me, is it true that you and Ricky have split up?'

She smiled and reached for the second bottle of Bordeaux. 'Here, have some more wine.' She winked at me and said, 'The night's a pup.'

～ ～ ～

The 'Meat Balls'

~

RAY DOOGUE

Looking back over the years I recall that many of the most interesting aspects of life in the sea were first pointed out to me by fishermen from other parts of the world. I was talking to a very knowledgeable American commercial fisherman one day, when he asked me, 'Do you ever see any meat balls out there when you are among tuna?'

He was drawing on his knowledge of what happened in the tuna fishing grounds of the Northern Hemisphere. He went on to explain that tuna rounded up masses of anchovies into tight circular balls by swimming around vast schools of these sardine-like little fish in ever-diminishing circles.

His question immediately sent my mind back to tremendous scenes of activity I had witnessed a number of times over the years. There had been glints of silver on the surface at such times, and showers of little fish leaping out of the water in a desperate attempt to escape. Predators, snapping at their tails, had often quite clearly been present.

My friend advised that I should look for such 'meat balls', as he so graphically labelled them, next time I was among tuna. Once I began looking for them it was remarkable how many of them showed up all over the sea.

A 'meat ball', or packed mass of anchovies, is really something to see. The first one I spotted after this discussion had a few sooty shearwaters (muttonbirds) hovering over it. They were sitting on the water with wings outstretched, ready for instant flight, and picking at objects in the water. We headed our boat towards the centre of the activity and cut the motor so as to drift into the middle of the disturbance without creating too much panic. Looking over the side, I spotted a large yellowfin tuna, swimming round on its side and looking up at us from a distance of about 6 metres.

As soon as we entered the disturbed area, masses of achovies clustered about our boat as they will around any floating object. We were able to dip half-buckets of anchovies out of these schools, the tiny fish so comatose with weariness that they made little or no attempt to avoid being scooped up.

This was not a very large concentration, but in subsequent days I was to see some enormous aggregations of sea life rounded up in this way. And what a sight it is to see. Gannets come rocketing out of the sky in perfectly controlled dive bomber action, closing their wings at the precise moment they enter the sea to knife deep down or to make a shallow dive to scoop up an anchovy near the surface. When the concentration is herded into an almost solid mass, the birds will merely sit on the surface feeding on the massed bait which is forced into a tight ball by the combined action of tuna, skipjacks, dolphin and many other forms of sea life.

A really big 'meat ball' is a sight to remember. Bonito whip around the outer edges of the school in a blur of indigo and big yellowfin tuna zip through the schools leaving an arrow cut-water in their high-speed transit. Often in the centre of such vast aggregations of bait, several large sharks will be seen lolling lazily, seemingly inhaling anchovies in much the same way as a child will suck sherbet.

The truly astonishing thing is the speed with which such a huge gathering of bait fish can be demolished. Every kind of surface-dwelling fish for miles around seems to zero in on such activity. It is simple to check what there is around by jigging a feather lure up and down near the centre of the activity. You may strike a yellowfin tuna, a big yellowtail, a kahawai, an albacore or a skipjack. Sometimes even bottom feeders, like snapper, will show up among the participants in the carnage.

One day we set a gill net for skipjack in the vicinity of such a congregation of bait. It was a very light affair, made from nylon monofilament and buoyed at intervals to hang deep in the water. Schools of skipjack swim straight into such nearly invisible nets and as the mesh interval is sized to allow their bullet-shaped heads through and then lock behind the gill covers they very quickly drown.

We had left the net set while we trolled round, looking for bigger game. Another commercial fisherman called the boat on which I was a passenger, saying that our net was sinking and we had better come back and have a look at it. When we reached the net and started to bring it aboard we saw fairly quickly the reason.

There had been some very large sharks in the 'meat ball' and they had obviously headed toward our net because the school dispersed when the bait was all gone. The first few metres of the net produced perhaps 20 skipjacks, but there were enormous holes in the net which suggested that something like a fleet of large trucks had passed that way.

Further along, we came on a bronze whaler which might have weighed 220 to 270 kilograms and which had further complicated the deal by rolling itself up in the net. Sharks invariably behave in this way: when in trouble they seem to react by spinning round. Often they roll up a steel trace and get it to the single line which they can break easily on their sandpaper-like hides.

It posed quite a problem to clear this brute from the net with the inadequate weapons we had at our disposal and by the time this fellow broke his way out to spiral back down into the depths the net was a complete ruin.

The reason why bait fish shoal in this way is not easy to discern. Obviously they haven't many options open to them when they are harassed from all sides by predators herding them toward the surface, while at the same time they are subjected to the attention of myriads of sea birds. Some, no doubt, escape to carry on the species. The astronomical numbers of these tiny creatures in the sea ensures their continued existence—until man intervenes to destroy the very last of the species in his greed for profit.

Most predators in the sea cease to kill as soon as their appetites are satisfied. There are some exceptions to this. The American bluefish, which is a very close relation to the Australian tailor, sometimes seen in these waters, is the only species I know of which seems to kill for the hell of it, leaving masses of dead or dying fish as it passes by.

'Meat balls' I have seen in our waters seem to be destroyed in their entirety. Only a few scales, twinkling like stars in the blue oceanic water, with some blobs of oil floating on the surface, remain to mark the scene of enormous activity mere minutes before. A few gannets and shearwaters, too heavy with food to fly off, swim lazily away from any approaching boat. Nevertheless, one feels that some of these little bait fish obviously do get away.

It has often been observed in nature that an attacker, given a potential of many victims, seems to become confused and is likely to miss out altogether. If you have ever watched a hawk diving on massed starlings you will know what I mean. For want of a better word this could be dubbed a 'confusion factor', provided by a beneficent nature to ensure that at least some are left to continue the propagation of any given species.

In recent years Peru has become the leading fishing nation of the world, mainly on the exploitation of the anchovy which breeds by the billion in the richly fertilised waters of the Humboldt Current. Each year about 4 million tonnes of pelagic fish, mainly anchovies, are turned into fish meal. In recent years a change in the flow pattern of the Humboldt Current has caused drastic results. The anchovies have largely disappeared. Probably the worst hit by this have been the millions of cormorants which live on the guano islands that make Peru the biggest exporter of phosphatic materials in the world. Hundred of thousands of the birds which produce this substance have starved to death in the absence of the anchovies.

Such are the riches of the sea that the enormous carnage of the destruction of a large 'meat ball', before one's very eyes in a few minutes, is not in reality the catastrophic event it might appear to be. It has been estimated that a single school of herrings might contain 3 million individual fish. There are many such schools in even a relatively restricted area of sea, so that the total number of herrings must reach astronomical totals.

To carry the comparison further let us consider the European catch of herring, which can amount to 20 billion kilograms in a favourable year. This is probably the merest fraction of those left in the sea, half of which, in theory at least, must be females, capable of producing $1\frac{1}{2}$ million eggs per year. Herrings are only a fraction of the total fish population in these same waters which might harbour billions of other fish of other species. The richness and tremendous population of the open sea beggars description.

The 'meat ball' made up of anchovies is not the only type that I have seen in these waters. Many years ago, before the Japanese cleaned out most of our marlin, it was not unusual to come across a 'golden ball' made up of koheru, a type of mackerel closely related to the horse mackerel.

The marlin seems to have gained an unusual reputation, earned or unearned, for sagacity in stalking its prey. Coming on a scattered school of bait fish, the marlin doesn't rush in like a terrier chasing seagulls on a wet playing field. A full circle round the dispersed mass of fish sends them together in the same kind of panic move as that made by the anchovies pursued by dolphin and tuna.

Two or 3 more turns about these massed bait fish brings the fish close together. When you look down into the water, the effect is precisely that of looking at a huge, golden globe. It is difficult to say whether the marlin are the only actors concerned in this kind of ocean drama, as I have seen mako sharks taken in the vicinity of such an aggregation of bait fish.

In the old days, such a sighting was taken as a sure sign of the presence of marlin. It used to be possible to take a marlin on the edge of such a concentration and lead it away so that the great mass of bait was not scattered. It has been said that 3 or 4 marlin could be taken without breaking up a 'golden ball', but the most I have ever seen taken in these circumstances were two fish in a double strike.

This phenomenon is certainly not restricted to our area of the South Pacific. I saw what I am sure was a 'meat ball' off southern Luzon in the Philippines when I was in those waters recently. Pacific Islanders round the Carolines know this type of concentration well, the only difference being that they call them 'rocks' not 'meat balls'.

Probably the story to end all stories of 'meat balls' was recounted to me recently by Iefata, an Ellice Islander who was a cadet officer on a ship on which I was travelling. On the island of Tarawa, which is famous in American stories of the Pacific campaign, about once a year fish of various types, weighing on average about 2.25 kilograms each, cast themselves on to the beaches in their thousands. As if to ensure that they become completely stranded, they leap on top of one another to make a heap about 30 centimetres high all along the tide line.

When I questioned Iefata, it didn't appear to me that they were herded ashore by dolphins or sharks. Iefata didn't attempt to find a reason for their actions. In simple, unsophisticated fashion he commented that we would probably laugh, but the elders of the population believed that it was a gift from God.

~ ~ ~

King Bait

~

KERI HULME

I think this season'll be the last, you know. Well, I mean, Coasters have their channels for spreading news, mainly ex-Coaster. From such people, news filters through to friends of ex-Coasters, not to mention relations, and eventually travels the length and breadth of the country. So maybe everybody knows why, and maybe everybody doesn't, yet.

Here I am, wound round in a welter of words, with a mystery on my hands, and very uncertain what to say about it. But this is the core of the matter, the heart of the nut: King Bait.

One thing everybody does know about the Coast is bait. Whitebait. That succulent little fish, quick and lucent, likened in an old haiku to the 'spirit of the waters'—

The whitebait:

as though the spirit of waters

were moving.

And every beginning spring, Coasters in their hundreds flock to the rivers and streams to swoop and scoop and blind-drag as many as possible out of sanctuary. When it's a good season, tons are lovingly packed into freezers against the lean, non-bait portion of the year; tons more are railed and flown over the hill, weekly. The Coast becomes a joyous place, the Coaster a contented being.

Of course, quite a few hundredweight get converted meantime into patties and omelettes and—well, whatevers. How did your mother cook them when she got them from the shop? I'm from Christchurch, we eke out the bait with flour and other foreign bodies. But here! Prodigality . . .

Take half a pound of bait per person, add an egg (two eggs, if you really like them), stir vigorously until fish and egg is a viscous froth full of strange little eyes. Add half a teaspoon of baking powder, a little salt, a smidgen of pepper, and fry the mix quickly, but with care. There you have a Coast feed, two right-sized whitebait patties, a subtly flavoured delight for anyone with a tongue in their head.

Last year, I missed the whitebait season. I was newly arrived from

Christchurch and, unaware of Coast ways, I bought my bait from a local fish-shop, and was well-content to get it 40 cents cheaper the pound than the family over the hill. Last year, I couldn't have told you the difference between a net for the Tere, and one used in the Grey. Nor what the advantages of supplejack over duraluminium. Set-nets were strangers, and the joys of very early morning tea in a tin shack on a river-side also unknown. The haiku was just a pleasant poetic fancy, blind-dragging was peculiar terminology and the great runs—well, myths of the past, a nice concept to beguile the tourists.

This year, I'm all enthusiasm. Buy myself the regulation round Grey net, and a bloody great pole to go with it. Equip myself with gumboots, get out old fishing clothes, and head down to the river at odd hours, waiting on changing tides. Drag that net, eyes strained, shoulders filled with a dead ache, hopeful of a nice little pudding in the bottom of the nylon bag. Or a very large one, for the season's started out a boomer. Tons of bait about. Happy faces all around, reflecting my smug grin. Full stomachs abounding, appetite satisfied, bankbook replete, and yet expecting much, much, more.

Things are just beginning. All over the Coast the hiss of hot fat and the crunching of little eyes . . .

And you know what? I thinks it's the end.

A very strange thing happened yesterday, twenty to nine under Cobden bridge; a strange, a horrible, a holy thing.

Friday night was a good night. I'd been to the local juicery, talked a lot, sung a bit, drunk to capacity, happy among happy people. Came home with the white moon high over the sea. A windless peace-filled night, the only sound that liquid continuous chirruping of tree-frogs. I cooked a couple of patties, ate them with a last cold beer from the fridge, and went to bed. Relaxed, full, content, perfectly at ease . . . ah, sweet.

And then, the morning. I woke suddenly, dropped abruptly out of sleep. For a moment I couldn't place the awakening factor, and then, there it was. A most peculiar hysterical liveness, filling the quiet street, streaking up my quiet hill, a shrill cacophony of voices.

'Berloody kids,' I think, and go to turn over, back to sleep.

It penetrates then:

'Whitebait running WHITEBAIT RUNNING WHITEBAIT . . .'

The words and the strangeness were enough. I shot out of my bed, into my denims and T-shirt faster than it's said, grabbed my boots and the net, and screamed out of the door and down the hill far more quickly than I've ever done. In fact, I'd reached the bottom before I realised that I'd left the pole back in the house. Or asked myself why somebody should tell everybody about a good thing.

But the street is alive as never before. The old lady recluse, who's probably never seen the light of day outside for years, is standing there, mouth open, staring-eyed, looking shrunken and untidy on the footpath. The new family at the corner is running in a graduated straggle round the corner, all 11 of them. As they vanish, the bloke next door and his wife with the new kid rush out. He's got the net and pole, and she has one arm full of kerosene tins and plastic bags, and one arm full of baby, and I swear it's not the former she's going to drop. I don't wait round looking any more. Bugger the pole, I hive off through a short-cut down into Bright Street. And believe me, all ambulant Cobden seems to be there. I'm a heavy sleeper, late waker, and the street is now crowded with everyone before me, running, walking, staggering, hell for leather for the river.

Well, it's normally a 10-minute walk from my place to the bridge, but even with the crowd I make it in a 3-minute run. After getting through the lame oldies and slow small fry, it's much easier of course. There was the risk of being skewered by poles, or having the breath thumped from one by a carelessly swung kero tin. Christchurch Friday-night-in-the-Square experience came to the fore here, though, and I'm in the van of the rush as we reach the river, that stretch just before the north end of the bridge.

Down the bank, trampling bush, slipping, kicking someone, grazing my hand on a tree I use to break my headlong eagerness a moment. All pulsing wild excitement to get a spot.

And stop aghast. Because, before God, the Grey is solid whitebait, bank to bank.

A fabulous mass of life, so thick in the river that water isn't seen. Just a seething froth of bait, frantic yet purposeful, a live river flowing in from the sea. And the hiss of disturbed water from their passing is louder than rain, louder than rapids, as spirited and loud as great falls.

I scoop, holding the rim of the net. It's FULL, absolutely chokka, and I drag it, elated, to the shore. The nylon is strained to its limits. Damn, nowhere to put the catch! But the bait, contrary to the normal lively whipping efforts to get out of the net and into the river, lie there like a sacrifice, and peacefully begin to die.

Strange. All my feverish desire to catch whitebait is gone. I lay the net with gentleness on the riversand at my feet, and all along the bank, as the people come slithering excitedly down, and then stop, stunned, they are now doing the same. Over on the Greymouth side, the weird thing happens, as the crowds gather and swell and burst to the riverside. Horrified reverence for this impossible dream-run.

Except one man.

I don't know who he is, a thigh-booted dungareed individual, made distant and inhuman by his action. For he is swinging his net like an automaton, scooping the bait, flinging it silver and anywhere onto the shore. There is saliva hanging in a shining string from the corner of his mouth, and I am not so far away that I can't see the money-glaze on his eyes. It's inevitable, a feeling of disaster growing. Stop it you bastard, from voices in the crowd, leave them alone. But he continues shovelling up the unresisting harvest.

. . . an eddy in the river of bait, or an eddy of the crowd, pushing harder out? I don't know, but he is suddenly off his feet, falling with grotesque flailing slowness into the froth of eyes. The bait-river moves on, and how to swim when the water is gone, how to swim in a viscous moving jelly? His dark head is above the river once, shining all over with lucid bodies, mouth gaping open, nostrils flaring wide, but full of writhing fish . . .

If ever a man died in dream turned nightmare, that was him. And yet, not a movement or sound is heard from any of us. Just a shared feeling of wonderment, of rightness, and inevitability, as the whitebait we caught die on the shore. Things move to a conclusion.

And then there is an unforgettable sound, a vast wind of indrawn breath coming from the seaward end of the river. People astonished, bereft of all movement except the gasp of awe. Slowly it swells, welling along the banks of the river, both sides of the river, while we who have no knowledge, wait and there, midstream, lambent, borne on the living tide, the spirit of the waters, moving.

We disagreed how big today. Ten or maybe 12 feet of lighted perfection. Clear as the most clear water, except for the fine line of black speckling on his sides, and the slender dark-drawn rays of his 4 fins and tail . . . and the goldened brain in the top of his head . . . and the eyes, the great silver eyes, intensely circled black centre, burnished globes on the inward side of his head. They reflect neither intelligence nor love, nor malignity, but show forth pure being. Summation. A complete benign magnificence.

For as the multitude of whitebait had gathered to protect this one by sheer pacific numbers, so was there nothing to fear from him. Watch with calm incredulity as he passes.

King Bait.

And as much bait flowed behind in that protective solid wall, now unharried by fish or bird or man, as came to be preyed on before. I thought of the millions upon millions of ridiculous harmless little fish, who had been sacrificed to provide a safe passage for that majesty, and did not wonder much therefore at feeling echoes of their massed consuming joy.

There is nothing in the river, except the white slimefroth of their passing, and the water. And somebody says, loud in the quiet that follows after,

'Hell, I hope they make it to wherever that is going. I hope they get there.'
And somebody near me, voicing all the other thought of the people,
'God love us all, but are they ever coming back?'

~ ~ ~

Hint for the Incomplete Angler

~

KENDRICK SMITHYMAN

Not too far north from where I write set dawn
Before your bow precisely. Out there, cast
The kingfish from his feeding while you prey.

Smug blue worms will peck at your neat craft's side.
Show due respect then while you steal the tide.

There was a fisherman once who did things right.

For more than forty years he pulled fish out.
By line, net or pot God's plenty hauled to pout
And puff on the bottomboards, to smack
Themselves silly and die, or be tossed back
Until they swelled a right size for the pan
He kept on the wall by his sink. That man
Had long outgrown the truth of simple tales
Which said if he stroked his arm he showered scales,
That said for years he nourished an old mermaid
All to himself in his bach. Friend, he was staid,
Ordinary, and (it may be) none too bright,
But who could come godlike home with that high light
Morning on morning, to be sane as we
Would claim we are? Yet he did fittingly
More than we'd dream, and with more dignity.

For when he couldn't heave any more at the net,
When the old man snapper clung too hard, he set
His nose to the sea away out east of the Head
To give what was due from good years to the tide.

Watch for the worms as you go, at your dinghy's side.

~ ~ ~

Family Tradition

~

BOB SOUTH

As fathers so often do, mine introduced me to fly fishing—in northern California when I was 6.

It was a case of him desperately wanting to share the joys of the sport he loved with a young son not yet sold on the value of standing in freezing, waist-deep water casting imitation insects, or occasionally unwilling, wriggly worms or salmon eggs procured from a small jar, to unsighted fish.

It wasn't until many years later, when I also grew painfully keen to teach my own New Zealand son to fish, that I understood how important it is to share the ultimate fishing experience, and your boy's first fish, with him.

But how difficult it is to help your own kid—too young to drink, years from wedlock, and too immature to hunt—to comprehend the infamous Chinese proverb by which you live:

> *If you wish to be happy for one hour get intoxicated.*
> *If you wish to be happy for three days get married.*
> *If you wish to be happy for eight days kill a pig and eat it.*
> *If you wish to be happy forever learn to fish.*

You don't wait for a boy to understand that; you just take him fishing and hope he grows up to appreciate the ridiculous proverb as much as you do.

The meandering Waitahanui River 10 miles south of Taupo seemed the ideal location to start Jason fly fishing. He and his younger sister Julie had already landed ample numbers of trout, lead lining and harling near Stump and Tokaanu Bays. Actually, Julie usually caught the most by far from the boat. Talented girl that. And lucky! Pity she never showed much inclination to river fish.

But when Jason turned 11, it was time for him to be led to a river to catch a trout like a man—or so his father thought.

My oversized size 9, all-rubber Skellerup waders engulfed him. Only the odd tuck here, a discreet fold there, and a massive belt buckled tight around his skinny waist allowed Jason to keep the things up and on, and safe should he fall in.

We would wet fly for his first fish—at the accessible, popular and easily fished Crescent Pool—using a Green Rabbit. Simple enough.

Placed thigh deep in a gentle current, Jason excitedly fed out line without having to cast. As excitedly he gathered in flyline just as he'd been taught, slowly making the imitation sized 8 fly swim like a smelt. His technique lacked the stylish grace of more experienced adults. Nevertheless, his method—untidily stringing large loops in his right hand, rather than neatly figure-of-eight coiling in his palm—seemed efficient enough at first.

It wasn't until a 3-pound hen tracked the Green Rabbit nearly into his pocket, engulfed the fly and madly striped line from Jason's hand, that the large gathered, efficient-looking loops rapidly became larger knots.

Jason had hooked his own first fish on fly all right. But in doing so, he also collected a bird's nest that would have done nicely as home for any wayward South American condor.

Naturally, in stepped concerned Dad, ever keen to ensure son's first fish in a river remained just that, not, instead, one of those heart-breaking brief hookups and premature releases.

Now, Waitahanui trout, like most fish, are humourless and lack patience—they especially don't like sharp barbed hooks penetrating their soft, sensitive lips anymore than we do. But some hooked trout react differently and become so coy they can quietly stick around longer than expected—like the 7-pound monster I once witnessed a fishing companion hook up and later land in the Waitahanui's Pig Pool after all but the first 3 feet of his line and trace were wrapped in a mess around one wader boot. Remarkably, this particular suicidal jack swung off the end of my mate's boot, almost apologetic, until the line was casually cleared from his foot so the mighty fish could ever so gently be coerced ashore.

Jason's fish, however, wasn't to be as forgiving or intent on death as my mate's. While father and son struggled to undo the massive tangled web in Jason's hand, while father softly muttered expletives and son louder exclamations of dismay at the prospect of losing his first fish on fly, the trout merely tugged more and more belligerently in predicably valiant and violent attempts to take the entire cluttered mess through the eyelets and back to the lake in a bid to escape the entire tragic-comic escapade.

Eventually, with no sign of the massive knotted line clearing, the trout broke free, taking trace, Rabbit, and Jason's heart with him. Boy and man were left distraught and drained at the fiasco.

Further attempts that day, in the same pool and others on the gentle, meandering stream, lacked enthusiasm and proved futile. The heart, mind, and pride take time to heal.

It wasn't until the following year, during one of the first major May runs from Lake Taupo up another small river 15 miles north of Turangi that Jason and father redeemed themselves.

Fishing a bubbly run along the true left bank immediately downstream of the tiny Kahikatea spawning stream, Jason, now crudely proficient in casting short distance, landed 7 trout, all over 6 pounds, nymphing with weighted Hare and Copper flies.

Tossing his line upstream just where the Kahikatea emptied into the main river, Jason managed to guide his fly neatly through crowds of fish stacked up anxiously waiting to exit the main flow and get on with mating in the spring creek that was the Kahikatea.

Really, because of the numbers in this spawning run, these were genocide fishing conditions—the kind you strike once a blue moon. But the conditions seemed a justifiable reward for a boy who had waited more than a year to feel the weight of a terrified captive on the end of his line, and who had longed endlessly to beach his first river fish.

The joys of that freezing, overcast autumn morning were many. Listening to the deafening, echoing whoops of a delighted boy that accompanied every newly hooked trout, watching the nervous care with which consecutive fish were played and walked downstream through gentle rapids, before being side-strained to the bank. All these memories remain vivid, as fresh as the cold that tightened our faces that day.

What a reverse experience this had been to that miserable, gut-wrenching day on the Waitahanui.

Jason's absurd success rate on this river eventually tired or bored him, forcing him to take a break from hauling in fish. Such was the ease of hook-ups that day, though, on only his second genuine fly fishing outing, that it was perhaps fortuitous that he voluntarily withdrew and thereby ensured he didn't spoil the sport for himself forever.

Not yet such a fanatical convert to the sport that he might miss the subtleties which make fly fishing so pleasurable and addictive even without plentiful fish— the smooth unfurling of line forward and back, the delicate placement of line and fly on water, the mending of line to facilitate presentation, and, oh yes, the environment—Jason eventually handed me the rod in order that he might busily devote newfound energies to the construction of a miniature rock dam in the gravel bed to hold and keep his catch fresh.

As he gloated over his bag, it was a revelation to witness this boy, my son, and his first fish. Here was a child filled with himself, for the moment a master of his dreams. The instinctive feeling of compassion, even remorse, he probably felt for the fresh, silvery, streamlined torpedoes he had just caught and which now lay motionless at his feet was happily replaced by the pride which so visibly swelled in his chest and flashed on his face every time an equally proud father turned to shower glances of silent praise on him.

As he's grown older, Jason has continued his fishing when his lifestyle and work permit. No longer am I teacher and he pupil on the river. We fish as peers. He handles a rod with consummate skill, casts better than I, and invariably catches his share of trout. Now mostly we only find time to dangle lines together on special occasions when our lives cross paths. While many of our later adventures have produced memorable results, too, and while many of our hours on various rivers have ended in mutual fatigue and admiration, while we've laughed more at lost fish and whenever either of us has emerged soaked from falling in some river, while we've exchanged looks of awe at prize fish, even while some of our increasingly infrequent trips have those rare, quality experiences everyone cherishes, none—for me at least—has yet come close to the day Jason landed not his first fish on fly, but his first 7.

It was as if a generation of tradition had been successfully passed on.

∼ ∼ ∼

A New Perspective on Eels

~

JON GADSBY

They're pretty strange things, eels. You know, really strange. Old Snowy used to catch them—just like that, you know, with his hands. I mean just with his hands. He'd gut his fish in the water and wait. Soon the eels came round, and they always did, edging, gliding, shimmering in, out of the light so's you could hardly see them. Coming out of nowhere you'd think, but they'd always turn up. Vague black shadows in the water, angling in off the current like bad dreams. Well old Snowy was in just like a bloody heron.

Whack! One hand straight into the water and a finger through the gills. Arm waving like a windmill, and out would fly this big, black eel, behind him. Didn't pay to stand too close behind Snowy when he was eeling. There was a likely chance of wearing one of the big black slimy buggers round your neck, and shit, then Snowy would laugh. Laugh fit to bust a gut while you ran around screaming, trying to get this horrible thing off you. And Snowy's dogs bouncing all around your feet, tripping you up, and probably laughing too, and waiting for their chance to get at the eel.

Snowy's dogs bloody near lived on eels. He reckoned it was good for them. Full of iron, he reckoned. Well Snowy's dogs must have been bloody near full of iron as well, I reckon, the amount of eels they got through. He used to stew them up for them, in the old copper at home, chuck 'em out all steaming, and the dogs would be really into it. After a while he couldn't be bothered stewing 'em up any more so he just took them home in a sack and tipped them out by the kennels. Then after a while he couldn't be bothered doing that either so he just flicked them onto the river bank, and the dogs hoed in. Never seen anything demolish eels quicker that old Snowy's dogs. Ruined them completely, so his brother reckoned. They were good dogs too. The three of them'd take on a 300-pound pig, no trouble, till Snowy put them onto the eels. After Snowy died, his brother tried to work them with his own dogs, but he was shit out of luck. Every time they got onto a porker, Snowy's dogs'd hang around till the beast was secure, then bugger off down the river looking for eels. Or maybe they were looking for Snowy—I dunno.

But I never liked touching them. The eels I mean, not the dogs. Didn't mind catching them, but I'm buggered if I liked touching them. Catch them on a piece of string, and drag them up the bank, no trouble. Whack them with a hunk of willow or a bloody great rock. Poke them into a bag with a stick and take them home for some of the old people. They were always rapt. They didn't mind touching them. Watched an old guy skin one once. He nailed it—I'm not kidding—nailed the bloody thing to a tree, grinning all the while. He makes this cut just below the gills then he peels it, all the skin right down. Just like taking a sock off. Makes another cut with the knife, leaves the head hanging on the tree and takes this big, long, white fillet into his missus. She was rapt too, and had a skillet all going on the range, hot fat fairly smoking. In goes the eel in pieces with a coating of flour, and blow me if the thing doesn't come back to life. Wriggling all over the pan it was, and the old man and his missus laughing fit to bust. I had to excuse myself from that one. I've never liked the idea of putting anything in my mouth that moves.

Uncle Barry had a thing about eels too. Hated the bastards. I reckon it might be something hereditary. They take all the juvenile trout, he'd say. No they don't, I'd say back. I'd been to a talk the acclimatisation bloke was giving at the community centre. Eels are predatory on just about everything that's little, including other eels. But once trout get past the fingerling stage, they're sweet. Mind you, I don't think Uncle Barry even knew what a fingerling was. But there we were one day, down by the river in this really ace spot. A place I'd never been before, but Uncle Barry knew about it. There was a line of what looked like solid willows, but if you crawled through, a spot opened up that was just magic, with just enough room to cast. Deep water and weed beds in front of you, and a ripple flowing around a bend on the other side. I mean this was spot X for a fish. It even smelt like a fish—all damp and mud and wild spearmint. Flick your worm into the top of the ripple and just let it roll down around the corner into the deep water in front of you. That's where the big trout would be waiting. Just on the edge of the current. There was another bend and ripple just 50 yards below, so if you hooked into a fish you'd be able to follow it down there to land it.

Well Uncle Barry got into one straight away, a goodie too. But instead of heading downstream into the fast water like it's supposed to do, this thing charges straight at us into the bank and the weed beds. Well Uncle Barry's cursing and swearing and trying to get his fish to come out of the weeds, and that's when the eels started to appear. One at first, then another, and then two or three smaller ones. Then a bloody big one, all taking an extraordinary amount of interest in that patch of weed, 6 feet down, in which Uncle Barry's prize winning fish was lurking. Uncle Barry tries letting his line go slack, and then cranking up the tension again. That's generally a good way of gettig a fish off the bottom. Not this time. He tried walking right. He tried walking left. Still his fish wasn't going to move. He gave me this look which I recognised was going to be followed by a suggestion that I might like to get in the water and follow the line down with my hands, but no way. Not with those eels round. I was just about to find something urgent to do further back in the willows, like dig some extra worms, when I heard his line ping like a guitar string. Uncle Barry said something rude and when I looked up, all the bend had gone out of his rod. I reckoned it might be safe to take a look now, and sure enough there's just a piece of slack line waving around in the breeze, cut like you'd done it with a knife.

We both stood on the bank looking down into the weed bed, and I was about to commiserate, when bugger me if this eel doesn't swim past with Uncle Barry's fish in its mouth. Holding it sideways, just like a dog with a bone. The other eels were following it, looking sort of excited, but this thing just swims around, doing something like a victory lap, and then clears off back into the patch of weed. Well Uncle Barry's face was a picture. I mean he hated being beaten at anything, especially by a bloody eel. So he pulls this piece of willow down, breaks it off, gets out his knife and starts sharpening the end into a point. I'm going to get this bastard, he says. I wasn't that sure whether he was referring to the trout, or the eel, but I didn't have much choice other than to go along with him.

The eel, the big one with Uncle Barry's trout, nosed back into cover, with just its tail sticking out, fanning lazily in the current. Well Uncle Barry feels he's got as close to perfection as he's ever going to with his primitive weapon, and takes this huge lunge at the bit of the eel he can see. All hell breaks loose in the weed bed as the sharpened stick hurtles in to do its deadly work. There's a cloud of sand and mud and severed weed fronds, and eels taking off in all directions. We'll never know if he hit it. Then as the current cleared the mess away, up from the depths, slowly at first, and then faster as it rose to the surface, comes Uncle Barry's trout. I couldn't help but notice that it wasn't showing any signs of life.

'Shit,' said Uncle Barry, as an eddy turned the fish and took it out into the mainstream. 'I'll get it,' I yelled, and grabbed the landing net. I ran through the willows to a place where the bank levelled off, then jumped down onto the shingle spit. I could make out the fish in the current as it started to pick up speed, approaching the shallower, faster water. I splashed into the ripple, going flat stick, and bingo! Got the bugger, just as it came round the bend before the next pool. Uncle Barry was yelling something from up the bank, but I couldn't hear him for the noise of the water. Anyway, I was looking at the trout. It was dead you know, I could tell that. Not a kick in it. Dead as a door nail. And do you know, there wasn't a mark on it. Not a scale out of place. I mean it looked like you'd just caught it, which Uncle Barry very nearly had. And then I looked again and thought 'bloody hell!' Because both its eyes were missing. Yeah, gone. Other than that it was in perfect nick, apart from being dead. Gave me a hell of a shock. The eels had taken its eyes while it was hooked. Blinded it. And once it was helpless they were just playing with it like a cat with a mouse. That was a big trout too— nearly 3 pounds, cos we weighed it. We ate it too. Didn't see any reason to let it go to waste, just because the eels had got it for us. But they'd blinded it. Would you believe that? Gave me a whole new perspective on eels, that did. Really gave me the heebie-jeebies. I mean you don't think about eels deliberately blinding things, do you?

I thought a lot about my new perspective on eels that summer. I thought about it particularly hard when I jumped off the old bridge a couple of months later. There were a whole lot of us jumping off the bridge regularly since a flood had scoured out a really deep hole around the piles on the school side. Must have been about 10 feet deep and just ace for jumping into. Some of the older kids'd dive too but I was never into that. If I'm going downhill into deep water I'd rather go feet first. That's what I used to say anyhow.

Well, rumour got round that a big eel had come down with the flood and taken up residence in the hole underneath the bridge. It sounded a bit like the Billy Goats Gruff story to me, and I never believed it. All us kids used to really wind each other up about eels anyway, when we were swimming. Every few minutes some clown would yell, 'Look out, there's an eel after your foot.' It got to the stage where you didn't take any notice any more. Bit like the boy who cried wolf, I suppose. Aw, they set me up a beauty one day, knowing about my new perspective on eels. I'd just jumped in and popped up to the surface, when the guys on the bank yelled 'Hey!' Well I looked at them, but it turned out to be just a diversion to stop me seeing one of the other guys who'd swum across to the other side, and was sneaking up behind me. 'What?' I yelled back to them. 'There's a bloody great eel after you,' they yelled back. 'Aw yeah?' I laughed and started swimming lazily in.

Of course, what I don't know is that this other guy's dived under me while I'm distracted, and suddenly grabbed my ankle from below, in a vice-like grip. Hell, I bloody near had kittens on the spot. I got a mouthful of river and just about walked over the water, getting out of that pool, so they reckon. I must have hit the shingle like a water skier, and the other kids are falling about laughing, and then the guy who'd grabbed me staggered out laughing, and I bloody near whacked him. Then he started falling about laughing. And then I saw the funny side and I started falling about laughing as well. But shit, it gave me a fright. Didn't think I'd ever be scared of eels again after that. You know, sort of cured me.

Well a few days later—it was a really hot summer that year—we were down at the old bridge again, same sort of deal. It was my turn to jump, and off I went. Talk about your whole life flashing before you. In the second or so it took to fly through the air and hit the water, I looked down and there it was, right below me, large as life. The eel that lived under the bridge, and man it was huge. Looked like a fence post in the water, about halfway down in the pool. Well it was too late to go back, but I sure as hell tried. The other kids reckon I did a cartoon act like Roadrunner, trying to climb back to the bridge through thin air, legs and arms going like Wily Coyote, in an attempt to get away from that eel. But I was sort of committed. I hit the water and that was it. A flurry of bubbles and you couldn't see a thing. Then I was kicking for the surface praying. 'Please nothing touch my leg. Please nothing touch my leg. Please, please please.' It must have worked cos nothing did. But boy, did I get out to that bank quick! Never said a word about it either. Must have scared the eel off when I landed on its head. Eels don't like being jumped on much, no matter how big they are. I didn't go bridge Jumping for a while after that, though. Not until my nerves had settled down, and a couple of floods had come through to clean the place out. Even then, I always looked first.

Then Uncle Barry told me this story one night. He'd heard it from one of the shearers at the pub. They'd had wet sheep for two days, and this guy gets bored and decides to go fishing. Well he reckoned he'd seen the biggest eel. I mean like the biggest eel this guy's ever seen in his life. It was huge, he reckoned, and this guy was from up north, so that's saying something. He reckoned this thing must have been 7 foot long if it was an inch. 'Where'd he see it?' I asked, and Uncle Barry told me. 'We should go and have a look-see,' he said. And so we did, next Friday night.

I'd got the bus up from town and arrived just in time for Uncle Barry to knock off at the workshop. I dropped my gear off at the house across the road while he got out of his overalls, and we piled into the old Vanguard. Ten minutes later we were down at the place where the track ran out, on the riverbed at the back of Currans' place. 'I know the place he's talking about', said Uncle Barry. 'About a half mile or so downstream there's a fork with a big log-jam on the far side. It's made a pool and a backwater going right back into the willows . . . deep as hell. That's where he reckons he saw it.'

Uncle Barry disappears around the back and opens the boot on the Vanguard, and hell, what a stink. 'What you got there?' I said, holding my nose, as he wandered back around, holding an onion bag at arm's length. 'Yeah,' he agreed, holding his own nose and grinning. 'Went out to Bluecliffs last Sunday and got a few blue cod. Took the fillets off and chucked the rest in a bucket. Heads and tails . . .' he nodded at the bag. The stench was overpowering. 'You reckon they'll do the trick?' he asked. I nodded. Eels love rotting fish like starving musterers do the sound of someone banging a tin plate.'Good, you carry them then,' he motioned, handing me the onion bag. I didn't have the heart to say no . . . not with him going to all that trouble and everything.

I found that by tying a thin strip of flax around the neck of the bag, I could drag it a few feet behind us, and so try to keep it downwind. The stink wasn't so bad there. It mellowed out a bit after we'd crossed the river the first couple of times, and by the time we'd got down to ground zero, it had faded back to a dull rotten pong. This was it all right. A big tree had jammed smack across a side-stream. A flood must have brought it down and piled all the shingle under and around it until it was just like a dam. The water had backed up beyond into what must have been a cut that was there already from the old riverbed. It stretched back into the willows, still and black and deep. Quite a spooky backwater really. 'This is the place,' whispered Uncle Barry. 'This is where he saw it.'

We were standing on a spit at the end of a ripple which shelved off into the pool that fed the backwater. Uncle Barry took the stinky onion bag and placed it just on the edge so it hung down into the deeper water. He wedged one end of the flax string with a rock. The onion bag turned lazily in the gentle current, just enough to take the smell across the pool and back into the deeper water. We sat back to wait, leaning against the beached end of the log. Pretty soon the eels started arriving. It was amazing where they came from. One minute there's a clear pool, and the next, these shapes are drifting in, coming out of nowhere. Gliding in like miniature submarines to form a loose semi-circle, not quite in clear vision, around the area of the bait. As they got braver, the odd one would make a quick dash in, give the bag a shake, and flash back into the deep. We sat against the tree, still as death. Watching.

Uncle Barry saw it first. He nudged me and motioned ever so slightly with his head. I looked where he was looking. Couldn't see a thing. The light was just starting to fade, and all I could see was a sunken log where the pool shelved away. Must have been a piece off the tree we were leaning against. That'd been there all along, hadn't it? I looked at Uncle Barry. 'Whatta you mean?' I said, without saying anything. He nudged me again and I looked back. It might have been a trick of the light, but the log seemed to have got closer. Then I noticed it too. Very, very slowly, the 'log' was getting closer. And it wasn't a log. Shit, it was a size. Biggest eel I'd ever seen, that's for sure, and with a head on it like a bull terrier. It moved in, so slow you'd hardly notice. Still more of it coming and you couldn't even see its tail yet. The smaller eels got jittery and backed off, not that I blame them. And the big one—the monster—just hangs there. I could see its gill flaps working . . . see its eyes now . . . see its nostrils, and bloody hell, the thing had horns on its head! I'm not kidding you. Horns. Spikes sticking out, part way down the nose. That was one scary eel, man. I looked at Uncle Barry and he had a funny look about him. Just staring into the water. Then bang! So quick it gave us a fright the eel half turns over and charges in on the bag, faster than you can see. There's a swirl and a chatter of shingle as the flax pulls out from under the boulder. I'd swear I saw the thin end of a tail, still wide as a cricket bat, come out of the water. And then gone. The eel, the onion bag, the whole caboodle. The smaller eels came gliding in again from the outer edges, nostrils open and mouths questing for scraps. Uncle Barry just stared at the water for a while. Eventually he got to his feet, stiff from where we'd been sitting. 'I reckon a spear's the way to go,' he said.

~ ~ ~

Deep River Talk

~

HONE TUWHARE

It's cold: it's golden; a magnificent
orange disc playing peek-a-boo
from the far-side of straggly
strings of leafless rastafarian willows
on the other side of the river.
The river's wide here: it's

undecided: it's steeling itself
never to turn and go back uphill.
Steam's rising from it and it's
not the early morning sun that's
doin' it; I can't raise heat
from the sun yet.

The veins of the river are swollen.
They're bending to the tide's
up-swing: tempers are like sails
shredding in a gale.

There's talk of a merger. A know-all
insect on stilts has just walked out
on top of the waters to supervise
the talks; I suppose pretending
to be Jesus.

In the sunlight mullet are jumpin'
and making lovin' archways of silver
for the migratory ocean-seeking eels
eeling their way down down; down
to the river-mouth and away.

The river's pushy, 'Back off! Thus far
and NO further —'

'I'll see YOU outside, mate,' says
the sea, turning. A swish, a tiny
whip and swirl of water—

Snap!

Daddy-long-legs has joined his
ancestors by way of a hungry trout's
stomach & stomach-ejector.

Happens to people too, nowadays—with
sharks hangin' around a lot.

~ ~ ~

Calm

~

DAVE WITHEROW

Odd things happen that there is no accounting for. Take last Thursday, for instance, when I was driving through Southland with a bunch of the cobbers. It was a splendid morning, with a fine, brisk gale thrashing the willows and making us think about fishing. But we had a big order of dags to fill, and it didn't look like we'd get them before lunchtime. All the same we couldn't help having a look in the rivers as we passed.

There were a couple of Americans with fly rods on the bridge over the Mararoa, and we stopped for a word. They were in a vile temper. Came to New Zealand 6 weeks ago, they said, and still hadn't caught a trout. Well, they must have been pretty poor fishermen, because conditions were just about perfect —low water, with the wind still rising, and a good surface chop to hide the approach. Any mug could have caught a fish on a day like that, and we left them to it.

Te Anau was coming down with dags that summer, so we crammed the truck and shot off back towards Five Rivers, making good time with the help of a powerful tailwind. We might get some fishing after all, with the day still young and the Mataura just half an hour away. But there was something wrong, and it wasn't till we climbed over Jollie's Hill and were dropping down towards Parawa that the truth punched home—there was no wind.

We got out of the truck at the Angler's Rest, and the quiet stillness was eerie. There were no branches, or anything, flying through the air, and you could stand straight up, rather than leaning over to deal with the blast, and Albert was wobbling around like a drunk, getting used to the newness of it.

We had a cup of tea and got back in the truck and drove down the winding, willow-lined road to Nokomai. There was still no wind. There was silence everywhere and the grass in the paddocks was vertical. By the third bridge nothing had changed and Albert was getting nervous, but I decided to get out and have a look around anyway.

When I got to the river it was uncanny. The surface was flat and calm. There were no wind-lanes, or whitecaps, and you could see right into the water. You could see through the surface as if it didn't exist, and make out pebbles and leaves and sticks all over the bottom. It was weird, and I had never seen the likes of it before—although I remember my grandfather telling me years ago that when he was a boy something of the same sort had happened to him on the Oreti, close to Mossburn. The next bit you just won't believe.

I was leaning out over this gorse bush on the bank beside a big green pool. There were rocks and things and a beer bottle lying on the bottom of the pool, and I was trying to get into position to take a photograph.

Then, all of a sudden, here's what happened: I was looking at the beer bottle, thinking how peaceful it seemed, lying on the bed of the river, and it reminded me of other beer bottles I had known, and I went off into a kind of reverie involving beer bottles and even whisky bottles . . . and then a big trout stuck its head out of the water, and took a mayfly right in front of me.

I almost fell into the river. The mayfly was gone. All that was left where it had been were some little rings on the surface of the pool that widened out and vanished. I'm sure you'll think I'm making this up, but when the rings had gone the trout was still there. It was still right there, just under the surface, and I could make out every detail as though the water didn't exist at all. It wasn't moving its fins or anything, just hanging there, resting on the water.

It was a beautiful trout. There were vivid black spots on it, and red ones as well, and its whole body was a golden yellow colour, except for its back, which was brown. Its eyes were beautiful too. They seemed unusually alive and watchful, and one of them was watching me, so I hardly dared to breathe.

After a minute or two a purple mayfly came floating along, its little wings poised like a sail. The trout saw it and moved across underneath it, tipped its nose up, and that was the end of the mayfly—just some more rings on the surface.

During all this time there was no wind. The willow trees were not moving at all and it was so quiet I could hear a cicada barking two paddocks away. I watched till the trout took another mayfly, and then I crept away from the bushes and ran down through the sweet grass to the bridge. But when I got there the wind had come up at last, and I said nothing to the others for I knew they would never believe me.

They were happy. They were putting their rods together, laughing and joking in the freshening breeze, pleased that things had returned to normal. I put my rod up as well, and said nothing, and we went fishing.

∼ ∼ ∼

Copper Bracelet

~

JAMES NORCLIFFE

he could cast a line
smoothly exactly
at the moment
the gold weed parted
and a pool appeared

and could reel in furiously
the wriggling cargo

the caught butterfish
had fine green bones
and sweet white flesh

they had moved like shadows
beneath the swaying kelp

and he could move a scythe
smoothly easily too
like the smooth movement
of the kelp back and forth

the fine swaying stems
of the yellow broom
succumbed to the blade
and fell on to the loess terraces
in a wave of green shadows

the copper down
and brown dust
shone in the sweat
of my grandfather's arm

but how his green wrists ached

~ ~ ~

Wizard of the Waikato

~

JOHN PARSONS

Fifty years ago, fishermen were quick to respond to any bush telegraph signalling superb new fishing. Those who had their ears tuned to Taupo and Waikato ground, and who journeyed there at the loud, clear, and specific message of 1930, were not disappointed.

Among the first enthusiasts to arrive at the newly erected tented camp, lodge-building, and newly private water above Huka Falls, in November 1930, were Monty Tisdall and Len Isitt, two fishing friends who were to return time and again and, moreover, send many of their friends there.

Within a couple of months they were followed by a man who managed a more enduring medium of communication than a bush telegraph. F. E. Thornton, managing editor of the *New Zealand Fishing and Shooting Gazette*, came to test the mettle of the new so-called dry-fly water. The story he wrote in the February 1931 issue of his magazine is the first detailed account we have of the astounding fishing that was to be had on Alan Pye's Huka Lodge water.

Make no mistake, however: fishing of the same quality was present pretty well all the way upriver to Taupo itself. The only reason Thornton singled out the kilometre of Pye's water is easily understood by anyone who appreciates the often close connection between advertising and editorial columns in newspapers and magazines. For it was no coincidence that the issue of the *New Zealand Fishing and Shooting Gazette* in which Thornton's story appeared also featured a Huka Lodge advertisement.

If Pye hadn't advertised, it's likely that a picture of the Huka Lodge fishing as portrayed by a highly respected fisherman and fishing editor would not have been painted so early, so faithfully, and in such detail, for anglers and angling historians.

Although Alan Pye was an untried host, torn between all kinds of pressing demands, he wisely gave Thornton and the editor's companion, Jimmy, a great deal of time on that New Year visit. It was amply repaid. They even took photographs for the magazine, of Pye fishing, Pye sitting beside a bag of 16 good rainbows, and Pye netting a fish for Jimmy.

In the editorial of the issue in which the story appeared, Thornton reported that Messrs T.S. Withers, M. Tisdall, and Lieutenant Hogg, RN, had all enjoyed excellent sport at the fishing lodge. All fished with the dry fly and landed excellent baskets of fish from 4 pounds to 7 pounds in weight.

On the very next page, page two of the magazine, Thornton plunged into the story of his stay. It evokes an angler's paradise. Many were to follow Thornton into similar raptures, first with rod and then with pen, but though some could turn a phrase more neatly, few spoke with such authority.

On the experience of only one short visit, Thornton prophesied then and there that the Huka Lodge water was destined to become world-famous for its sport. He was so right. He quickly discovered that even in daylight large rainbows rose to the fly. From sundown to long after midnight every fish appeared to leave the centre of the river for the bays and runs close to the bank, where they plopped and gurgled as they sucked down floating flies, within easy casting distance.

He made it quite clear to his readers that the fish were real fish. Giants going up to 12½ pounds had been taken there on the dry fly. All his readers' skill, he told them, would be required to bring them to gaff on the fine tackle they must use.

He spent the first afternoon inspecting Pye's water, and reported that the Waikato there ran deep and ever clear. Some idea of the flow and magnitude of the river might be imagined from the fact that it was the outflow from Lake Taupo and thus its volume was equal to that of the Tongariro, the Tauranga-Taupo, the Hatepe, Waitahanui, and the dozens of other smaller streams and rivers that entered the lake.

No pen-picture, he said, could convey its loveliness as it gradually gathered speed to plunge over the sheer drop of the Huka Falls and roared and boiled and swirled on its way to the magnificent Aratiatia Rapids before sobering down to the flow and easy surface of a mature river winding its leisurely course for hundreds of miles to the sea.

The angler's first impression on beholding a river 6 metres or more deep at its bank was that it was some great angling joke to call the water dry-fly water. It was deep. It shelved steeply to the centre as clear as gin, with not a fish in sight.

Even as he wondered where a man could fish the dry fly there, up flashed a silver rainbow of 5 pounds from a rock shelf beneath his feet and seized a fly on the water.

Alan Pye had already cleared casting stands at favourite lies and pools. Any one of them—at Loafer's Pool, Picnic Point, or Lady's Pool, for instance—was enough for an evening's sport—such sport, wrote Thornton, as surely no other water in the whole of the world could give.

Right on schedule the first evening the fall of spinners and hatch of large sedge started. The whirling battalions of flies gave due notice of the amount of material for the rise to come, a rise which was not spasmodic or sporadic as on rain-fed or snow-fed rivers. The rise of fly and rise of fish were as much a daily part of the Waikato there as the clarity of the water. This could be understood from the peculiar local conditions, where floods or sharply varying temperatures were unknown.

With their tackle rigged, Thornton and his companion took their stand in time to see the advance-guard of the army to come—the small fish of 30 centimetres or so that broke water in countless numbers as the spent flies sank to the surface.

Thornton watched enthralled, and mounted a No. 12 Coch-y-bondhu to pass time with the little fellows till the main army arrived. A sullen plop close in indicated a weighty fish. The widening rings of its rise made a lovely target for the fly, and a quick switch scored a bull. An instant response came in a big black neb, and Thornton's fly disappeared in a swirl.

His first amazement was succeeded by a feeling of dismay, his reel shrilling in a high minor key as the fish ripped off line and still more line. But the river was clear, the small hook held, and the descending chromatics of the reel's music soon told Thornton that he had the fish in hand. He gradually wore it down till it was done.

Then a difficulty arose. For many years he had never used a net or gaff. If the fish could not be beached he gilled them by hand. But no such tactics would do with 10 metres of water beneath. He yelled to Jimmy in the next pool. Jimmy had a borrowed gaff, and he quickly appeared with it out of the scrub.

A moment later Thornton's first Waikato rainbow on dry fly lay on the bank, a glittering beauty of steely silver, faint crimson, and dark olive. Five pounds of concentrated virility, plump, deep, and a joy to the eye of any angler, no better fish could be desired.

They changed then to the special flies with the larger hook for secure holding. The moon rose bright and clear and the wonderful rise went on and on, dozens of fish rising everywhere around them. By 12.30 am they had had enough. Sixteen good fish lay on the bank, and as many more had come unstuck.

They sauntered back to the lodge at 1 am, musing on the river's topsy-turvy dry-fly fishing: a river 6 metres deep and more; fishing in the dark; big rainbows taking the dry fly. Thornton's world, at least, was all upset.

But stranger things were to come: they found Alan Pye back home too, stripped and floating in a hot pool—the Venus Pool at the lodge—enjoying a natural hot bath at 1 am, while 6 metres away the icy waters of the Waikato swept seawards, and in the small channel joining the two the glittering sides of golden carp reflected the pale moonlight as they swam in groups.

Looking back on his experience at Huka Lodge, Thornton saw it in its true perspective as something utterly new, absolutely unique, and an experience that no angler should miss. Delightful surroundings, wonderful angling, sightseeing, handy to Wairakei's weird collection of thermal wonders, it seemed to him that here was the angler's paradise so often dreamed of.

What amount of fishing the stretch would stand was problematical, thought Thornton, but it seemed fairly certain that fish replenished their numbers from the lake, for as the rainbow headed downstream they came to the impassable fall. It appeared impassable to him, although he heard from an authority that there was a strong suspicion that some fish did go over the falls and survive.

If that was right, said Thornton, proof was wanted. Until, say, a tagged fish was caught lower down the river the falls certainly appeared to be an impassable barrier. But there was no gainsaying the enormous head of fish resident there. Within a fair fly-cast from the bank one night, Thornton counted 34 fish rising.

He suggested that any visiting angler might stay either at Taupo, Wairakei, or the Huka Lodge. Personally, he said, he would go no farther than the lodge. Alan Pye was a fisherman himself; in fact of all the anglers he had ever watched, he doubted if there was a more finished caster anywhere. The man knew what anglers wanted. The outlook was beautiful, food excellent, and served to suit the rise. The hot pool was next to the sleeping quarters, and refreshed jaded muscles after strenuous exertion. The water was not 20 metres from the lodge, and on the lodge property fishing was reserved for guests alone, although the other bank was open to all.

Thornton recommended a rod between 9 and 10 feet weighing $6\frac{1}{2}$ to 8 ounces, the reel should contain 100 metres of dry-fly line, tapered or parallel to suit the angler's taste. Casts had to be fine, but of the very best quality, tapering from about $\frac{1}{4}$ drawn to 1x or 2x.

The flies, he wrote, were special flies on the model of those made by Captain Richardson, the discoverer and originator of the method of fishing in the water, and were known generally as Captain Richardson's flies. They could be obtained from Mssrs Tisdall, the CAC, and Ross of Napier, and locally from Loughlin of Taupo.

Those that Thornton himself used were samples forwarded by Ross, and he found them excellent in every way, while those he saw used from Messrs Tisdall produced equally good results.

Line, cast, and fly, he said, should be greased with Slideline, Cerolene, Nipigon, or some such waterproofing medium to make them float.

Given such an outfit, he said, it was merely a case of putting the fly in front of the fish, 'and then would follow the fight every angler dreamed of'.

That article is of absorbing interest for anglers who fish at Taupo. It paints a picture of an era they will not see again, unless by some minor miracle the caddis-larvae of the Waikato re-establish themselves, restoring dry-fly fishing to a river from which it was taken in 1941 by the North Island's need for water-generated electricity.

Thornton's accolade set the tone for practically everything else that was written of the lodge fishing. And there was plenty of it. Oddly, not a great deal appears to have been written up to the time that the gates controlling the out-flow from Lake Taupo were installed. But many mentions occurred later, especially after the end of the Second World War, in 1945.

Thornton wrote chiefly about the fishing, but Vincent Freeth, 5 years after Thornton, wrote chiefly about the man Alan Pye. Freeth, brother of the then editor of *The Press*, Christchurch, Hugo Freeth, wrote an article for his brother which he called 'Wizard of the Waikato'—and which he claimed was the first true fishing story ever told.

It was a filmy picture of Alan Pye he wrote, and also of Alan Pye's lodge on the wonderful Waikato above the Huka Falls. Anglers came to Alan to do him homage, he wrote. They came from the 4 corners of the earth—from the British Isles, from Ceylon, Africa, India, the Malay States and the Americas. And yet the man had no arrogance, no love for cities, no lust for power, but a heart full of kindness and a soft Irish voice that would charm a sigh from the heart of a gargoyle.

His realm was a kilometre of the most perfect dry-fly water in the world. Six to 10 metres of deep blue and green perfection it flowed; in quiet pools, in great whirls, in mad rapids. Because the Waikato was fed by the vast waters of Lake Taupo it never flooded and was the ideal home for trout. It sheltered thousands of fighting rainbows, up to an occasional 12 pounds or more, which rose to the dry fly at all hours of the day and night.

Freeth said that to see Alan fish that water was like having a great master tug at your heart-strings with the song of his violin. He lured the giants from their lair with the whistle of his poetic rod. His fishing was something to dream about in dozing before the fire on long winter nights.

Freeth couldn't say how Alan Pye did it. It was one of those things you couldn't explain: the swing of a Bobby Jones, or the dancing of a Pavlova.

When Alan switched his rod the heart stood still with anticipation, and when the fly lighted on the water it was with the saucy provocation of a practised flirt. He believed Alan when he said that presentation was 90 per cent of success in fishing. And so it was in life. But men and fish liked to be fooled by some men more than others. There lay the genius of deception.

But there was more to Alan's fishing than the pretty lie of the fly. He knew just where every fish of importance was in the river. Freeth swore that Alan knew what trout thought about and why they did this one day and this another.

Alan's own record fish at that time assumed, because it took refuge in gin-clear water, that it could tell a lie from a fly when it saw one. And yet the monster was undone one midday in brilliant sunlight. A gentle breeze betrayed it, ruffling the water and spoiling its judgment. Alan had waited for that zephyr for weeks. He crept down to the edge of the water and dropped a flippant fly on the ripple far out. The trout had almost decided on its siesta, but out of one sleepy eye all it saw was a fat fly. The ripple blotted out the betraying cast.

The fish hurled itself at the fly, and for the next 45 minutes fought for life in great leaps, lashing at the cast with its tail, all to no purpose.

It was just little things like that made Alan the angler he was; and you and I, said Freeth, the fishermen we are not. Or perhaps a man did know what fly was hatching each night and morning, and whether it was male or female, and how long the hatch would last, or whether fish laugh at fishermen and why not? In which case Freeth apologised to his reader, who would be one of the high priests of angling.

Freeth wanted to portray the Alan Pye he saw one evening on his arrival at Huka Lodge. Putting his head into Alan's cubbyhole, he found him absorbed in tying flies for the evening rise. There was time to mark his strong Irish face surmounted by a mop of fair curly hair.

'Tena koe, Alan,' said Freeth.

Alan looked up. 'For the love of Mike it's himself . . .' he exclaimed. 'By the Lord Harry, why didn't you say you were coming? It's the divil's own luck that I can put you up at all.'

Freeth, in one excited breath, asked after Mrs Pye, of Cuthbert the man-killing fish, and Muriel the milch-cow that almost invariably accompanied Alan to the river. And there was Alan's setter, Major, thumping a welcome on the floor of the verandah.

Before dinner they dropped down to the river to see Cuthbert the man-killer. They stood at the edge of the stream. Alan threw a titbit into the current. With a great crash a monster rainbow hurled itself from the depths, taking the offering in one great leap and descending again to the bed of the river where they could see his sinister shape alert for another morsel.

His tail moved swiftly as he poised himself against the current, said Freeth, and you could believe all the woeful tales that were told of him. His father, Freeth suggested, must have been the taniwha, the fearsome man-eater of Maori legend.

Patiently Alan waited for Freeth to ask if he had any objections to his clicking with Cuthbert. He did so in all innocence.

'Help yourself,' said Alan. 'That divil knows more than any man. He's broken tackle that would buy a king's ransom. What chance have you or I against him? Many a good angler has hooked him, but he won't budge an inch upstream. He just makes for that big rapid down yonder and you may as well be hooked on to an express train for all the good it will do you. Don't try him or he'll ruin you.'

They dined early, put their gear together, and went upstream. Muriel the cow and Major the setter accompanied them as of right. When the Irish move, observed Freeth, their animals go with them.

They sat themselves down on a grassy bank at Picnic Point opposite the tall cliffs. In the gold of the sunset they smoked in deep contentment, awaiting the magic fall of night and the miracle of a tumultuous rise. With a little imagining, Freeth could picture it as the crescendo of an orchestra. The tiddlers rose close in with the soft pluck of muted strings as the last gold touched the water. Dusk fell slowly, and heavier fish chimed in a little further out.

As the moon began to peep, silhouetting the dark cliffs, the giants rose with a deep cello note on the edge of the heavy current in midstream. The birds were then quiet in sleep, and in the hush of the night the river sang its age-old lullaby.

A great trout breaking the water in midstream was Alan's signal for action. His rod whistled once, twice, in the shadows away from the tell-tale moon. For one brief second before the rainbow struck, the fly sat like thistledown upon a streak of silver water. The line tautened, the reel screamed in the ecstasy of battle. The big fish headed upstream then came down again in a great leaping run.

Changing its tactics, it made towards them. Alan reeled in quickly, keeping tension on the line, but the rainbow was away again a flash, with the rod bent in a half-moon. Then, as that magnificent fighter felt the touch of the master upon it, it slowly yielded. The net passed quietly under its beautiful pink and silver body.

As the larger fish began to rise closer in the two fishermen separated, each to fish alone. At 10 o'clock, with more than a dozen betweeen them they clambered home with their bag. Then, a few metres from the lodge and the river, they plunged into the soft warm glory of a thermal bath under a canopy of stars—and so to bed . . .

～ ～ ～

My Late Father

~

KEVIN IRELAND

The evening before he remarried, my father went fishing. For several days there had been easterlies, which blew in hard on our part of the harbour, and that meant it was too rough to take out our 10-foot dinghy. Then suddenly the wind dropped and the sky cleared. As always, after a storm from that quarter, lines of long slow rollers would swell then thump with a booming echo against the beach.

My brother and I discussed the matter seriously and decided that going fishing was a funny item for someone to put at the top of a list of things to do before getting married. We agreed we couldn't work Dad out, but I was 13 and Athol, my brother, was 10, so we had only just begun to dwell on the mysterious ways of grown men.

Normally, we would have been invited to go along, too, so Dad's strange fishing expedition became even more peculiar when he asked us just to give him a hand to carry the oars and the anchor and the fishing gear down to the beach, and to help drag out the dinghy.

He said he was only going out for an hour and wanted to be alone. He would be back at half past 6, just as it would be getting dark, so he told us to be waiting when he came in, to grab the boat and clean the fish, if he caught any, because he had to be at Catherine's parents' place for tea at 7. Catherine was to be our new mother and the wedding ceremony would be on their front lawn.

We recited the instructions we'd been given as soon as we got home, for Catherine had dropped by to make sure that all her arrangements were not going to get mucked up at the last minute. She was only too well aware that the man she was going to marry had two serious problems. The first wasn't too difficult to put up with—it was just a common enough obsession with fishing— but the other was the kind of kink that could drive anyone crazy. My father was late for almost everything he ever did. He regularly missed buses and ferries, and he usually failed to turn up on time for appointments. If, by accident, he happened to be early, he would find something to do to make himself late. He didn't just apply himself to being late; he was a genius at it.

Which is why, when Athol and I went down to the beach at half past 6, we knew with absolute certainty that there wouldn't be a dinghy anywhere in sight. For a while we didn't bother too much, but just hung about and waited. Then we got a bit bored, so we walked up and down the beach, peering out to sea in the dim evening light, and listening, in between the rhythmic crunch of the rollers, for a call or the squeal of oars in the rowlocks.

It got dark quickly. There was no moon, but the stars were as hard and sharp as broken glass, as they always seemed to be after a storm. The sea turned black, and soon only the foam of the waves picked up the silver glitter of the night sky.

Then, possibly a bit after 7 o'clock, Catherine appeared out of the darkness. She had a torch, which she shone up and down the beach, as though she expected to summon our father out of the darkness. 'Where is he?' she demanded.

'He's late,' Athol said bluntly. He hadn't yet acquired any useful conversational frills.

'As per usual,' I added, trying to sound as though this was a sufficient explanation.

'Well, he was supposed to be back half an hour ago,' Catherine said. 'He knows we've got to go out.'

Athol and I kicked at the sand with our bare feet. 'He'll be in any minute,' I said. 'He'll have to come in. It's pitch black out there and he hasn't got a light.'

As soon as I'd finished, I knew that I'd come out with the wrong thing, so it didn't surprise me when Catherine snapped, 'Why didn't he take a light? That's stupid. He shouldn't have gone out without one.'

'You've got the only torch that works,' Athol said.

Catherine switched the torch off, as if she'd been doing something wrong, and cast us into deeper gloom. For a minute or so we couldn't even see the foam of the waves.

None of us spoke, until eventually she said quietly and steadily, 'It makes you wonder if you're doing the right thing, doesn't it? It calls everything into question. It forces you to consider whether some people actually believe fishing is more important than anything else in the world. More important even than getting married.'

There was a second pause, then she went on, 'Anyway, I'm not waiting around here and getting upset. I'm going back to the house. It's simply not fair.'

The moment she went, Athol and I decided to walk the full length of the beach. We didn't discuss what Catherine had just said, because we needed a bit more time to come to terms with it, so instead we talked about the darkness and how Dad might have made a mistake and come in somewhere else along the coast—though neither of us really believed what we were saying, and Athol closed the whole topic by telling me he didn't like the idea that it was so black out there that Dad might have lost his bearings.

It must have taken us at least half an hour to cover the whole beach, and while we did so, we discovered a strange thing about the light. Because the stars reflected directly on the sea, if you were actually in the water as you strolled along, you could make things out a lot clearer. You could observe how the rollers rose in low black walls against the night horizon, and then you could pick out a hollow curve as they came in towards you, before toppling over in a cascade of foam. It was quite different from standing up on the beach and trying to gaze into the void until your eyes ached.

'Of course he can bloody-well see out there,' Athol decided. 'So he couldn't have got lost, could he? He's just decided to keep on fishing and to hell with going around to the old bastards' place.'

'Don't swear, and don't be stupid,' I said. Some of the things my younger brother came out with made me really angry. 'They're throwing the wedding tomorrow. You know that. It's on their front lawn. He's got to go and see them.'

'Why?'

'You know why,' I tried to explain. 'It's the done thing.'

'Huh,' Athol said in disgust. 'If it was me, I wouldn't bloody turn up either. They don't want him in their family. Not really. I'd go fishing and stay out all night, too.'

'You know it's not like that,' I said. 'He's just late—he's always been the same.'

'Not like this,' Athol announced. 'It must be bloody midnight.'

'You're a nutcase. It can't be more than about 8,' I told him. Athol had no sense of time, as well as all the other things that irritated me about him. He didn't seem to realise that by exaggerating he was making everything seem much worse. There and then I decided I'd punish him.

'Do you want to know something really weird?' I asked, in what I hoped was a hoarse and spooky whisper.

'What?'

I couldn't see the expression on Athol's face, but I knew from the sound of his answer that he was expecting something he mightn't want to hear.

'When someone's *late*, it can mean they've croaked it. Late means they're dead.'

'I know that,' Athol said uncertainly.

'Well think about it,' I told him. 'When you're dead you're called the late Mr So-and-so. It's like this—suppose your name was Mr Early, and you were dead, they'd have to call you the late Mr Early. Get the idea?'

'Dad's name isn't Early. It's Green. Same as you and me,' Athol replied.

Sometimes he was distinctly lacking in savvy and imagination.'Anyway, he's not dead, he's out fishing.'

'All I'm trying to tell you is, he mightn't be early, but he's certainly late. I'm not suggesting anything else. So just pay attention, okay?'

It was a pretty nasty game I was playing, and all I can think all these decades later, as I look back, is that my own nerves must have been pretty frayed. Catherine had just been having second thoughts out loud about the wedding that was supposed to take place the very next day, and I was becoming increasingly apprehensive about how, whatever happened, our lives were certain to be changed. And all the time, nagging away at the back of my mind, was a terrible awareness that Dad was late on a dark night, and there were only our voices to keep us company as the rollers drummed against the beach.

I began to wish that I hadn't said the stupid things I'd just come out with, when we were spared the possibility of Athol's tears by the light of a torch coming towards us. It was Catherine again, and she'd brought us a piece of cake and a pullover each. We hadn't realised we'd got so quite cold till we began to feel warm again.

'Are you feeling okay?' I asked her after she'd finished cross-questioning us about whether we'd been paying attention and keeping a proper lookout, and if we'd heard anything.

'Of course I'm not,' she said—and she sounded it. 'I'm worried sick. He's two hours late. What could have gone wrong? There's no wind. It's not rough. And the breakers aren't very big.'

'I wish it was daytime,' Athol replied. He was trying to be a big help and making things worse as usual, and he'd completely missed the fact that Catherine wasn't wondering any more about whether she'd made a mistake in wanting to marry our father. She was temporarily past all that.

'Perhaps we ought to phone the police,' I proposed.

'A policeman on a bicycle?' Catherine said.'What could he do?'

This was long before the days of helicopters and fast police launches and cell phones. In those days the only telephone we had access to was a public callbox at the top of our road, and our local constable lived more than a mile away.

I shut up, but a couple of minutes later Catherine made me feel important by saying,'I think you've got something, Rob. I ought to drive around to the station and tell him. He might come up with something.'

'What about collecting a pile of driftwood first, and lighting a fire?' Athol suggested, and made me wish I'd thought up the idea.

'We could get a good blaze going,' I added straight away. 'You'd see it right around the harbour. It'd be like a beacon.'

'Good boys,' Catherine said. 'I knew there was something practical we could do.' And she shone the torch, while Athol and I dashed around and gathered a heap of wood from just above the high-water mark. I found some old papers and a magazine, which we tore up, and—just as I expected—Athol magically produced a box of wax matches that he was banned from carrying around. Dad had called him a young pyromaniac and had warned that if he ever found another wax match in his pockets, after the last patch of gorse he'd set fire to, there would be hell to pay.

The tide was going out, so we set the fire well down the beach and we soon had flames shooting up into the air, lighting the whole place up. We chucked a few large broken branches on top to keep it going steadily. For a few minutes the sight even cheered us up.

'He'll see the fire,' I told Catherine. 'He couldn't miss it from miles away.'

'*Miles* away?' She repeated. 'What are trying to tell me? He went out just off the beach. He wasn't going miles away.'

'I didn't mean that,' I explained. 'What I meant was . . .'

I stopped in confusion, but Athol got in quickly. 'Rob never knows what he means,' he explained. 'He talks without thinking. Like all that stuff about the late Mr Early. Ask him.'

'What's the time?' Catherine asked, cutting through our nonsense before I could retaliate by raising the subject of Athol's box of matches.

'It must be 9,' I told her.

'Then that's it. I'm going for the police. Even if it's just to give me something to do.'

She stayed long enough to help us stack more wood on the fire and to tell us to keep a sharp lookout, and she had just begun to walk away, when Athol suddenly jumped up and down, and shouted, 'I heard something. I tell you, I heard something.'

Catherine turned, then ran over to Athol and clutched hold of him, as if he had some sort of secret possession.

'I heard something again,' he yelled.

Together, we all walked quietly away from the fire and stepped out into the water, careful not to make splashing noises. Then we all heard the sound. It was a voice calling very faintly, just before a wave broke and obliterated the sounds. But we definitely picked up a 'Coo-ee', followed by an 'Oy'.

We all began yelling, until Catherine ordered us to stop. 'He won't hear us,' she said. 'Wait till the next wave has broken, then I'll count to 3 and we'll all shout 'Oy' together.'

We did, and we got another 'Oy' in reply. This time it was a little louder.

'Can you see him? Is he swimming?' Catherine asked frantically. She was up to her knees in the water by now.

'He's in the dinghy. Over there,' Athol shouted, pointing frantically. 'I saw him first.'

On the crest of a roller, outlined darkly against the stars, then suddenly glowing as it caught a faint light from the fire, I could make out the white shape of the dinghy. For some strange reason, it didn't come on in, but sank out of sight again, as if the sea had swallowed it.

We all began to shout again, and we heard another 'Oy'. Then the dinghy rose on another wave. It hadn't come much closer. It seemed to be glued out there.

'What's wrong with the boat?' Catherine yelled. 'Has it hit a rock? It's not moving.'

'There's no rocks out there,' Athol said, and as he spoke the dinghy rose on another wave and moved forward slowly, with Dad rowing like crazy. Then mysteriously, instead of surfing in towards us, the dinghy disappeared again as the wave broke.

'He's towing something,' Athol said. 'It's holding him back.'

Once more the boat rose, and the same thing happened. Athol and I were soaked as we tried to get out through the waves and take hold of the bow or the anchor warp. Then, as a second roller rose behind the one on which the dinghy seemed for a moment to be perched, we saw the dark shadow of a sea monster.

Suddenly Dad shipped the oars, stood up and leaped into the water, clutching a handline. 'Grab the boat,' he yelled, as the next wave picked the dinghy up and sent it careering towards us. It spun sideways and nearly capsized, but we grabbed it and dragged it to the beach.

'You should see the bloody monster,' Athol yelled, and for once Catherine didn't tell him off for swearing. 'He's hooked a bloody whale.'

Catherine said something, but neither of us heard, for we both dashed back into the sea and caught hold of Dad. He was easing the fish in, wave by wave, so that the weight of the back-surge wouldn't break the line, and each time the fish rose with a new roller we could make out its huge shape.

'It's a shark,' Athol decided. 'It's got to be a shark.'

'Take the line. Both of you,' Dad told us. 'And don't pull too hard. I'm going to grab it by the gills, or I'll lose it in the surf.'

It seemed a wildly dangerous thing to do, but it was his fish and there was no stopping him. He went out into the waves and lunged at the huge black shape. For a moment he seemed to be wrestling with it, then he moved towards us, waist-deep in water, dragging his catch with him.

Athol and I kept hold of the line and walked backwards to the beach. Then suddenly Dad half-lifted the monster and brought it up onto the sand by the fire. It was longer than the dinghy—except that it wasn't a fish at all. It seemed to be just a gigantic straggly heap of seaweed.

'Biggest kingie I've ever seen,' Dad said. Then he parted the huge bundle of seaweed, and suddenly we saw the long and lovely silver bulk of a giant kingfish. 'It's towed me up and down the harbour for 3 hours. I just managed to hang on to it with one hand while I pulled in the anchor with the other. It took me wherever it wanted. I've been for the ride of my life. It was like an outboard motor. It went crazy.'

'I thought you were drowned,' Catherine said. 'We've missed dinner. I don't even know if we ought to . . .'

She didn't finish the sentence, for Dad put a wet arm around her and gave her a kiss. 'I've always wanted one of these, and the Gods have given me one for a wedding present,' he said.

She didn't complain about his wet arm, but began to tell him, 'Well, at one stage I had to think I'd made a mistake and there wasn't going to be a wedding at all . . .' Then she stopped and her voice changed completely. She said, 'All three of you will catch your death of cold. Bring that fish up and have a hot shower, and get changed. I'm going back to get some cocoa on.'

We hauled the dinghy to the tree where we always chained it, then Dad slit the fish open and ripped out the guts and gills. Even standing by the fire, Athol and I were shivering, so we were glad to head back again. We picked up the oars and the anchor and the fishing gear, and set off. We had become part of the glory of it all, just by being there and helping. The only thing we were sorry about was that it was so dark that none of the neighbours could look from their doors or windows and witness our triumph.

That night, when we had washed and got into our pyjamas—and the next morning, too—we ate giant kingfish steaks. But we had to give away most of the fish to friends. Dad and Catherine went off on their honeymoon, and Athol and I had too many sausage rolls and cakes at the wedding to bother about eating again that night.

The extraordinary thing, it now seems to me, is that no one thought of taking a photograph or of trying to weigh the fish. So my father's giant trophy exists only in memory, in the shape that first amazed me, when it rose on the rollers, twice its real size, in a cowl of dark seaweed.

It will always be the biggest fish I have ever seen, and often when, for no particular reason at all, I remember my late father, I see him bending to a dark massive raggedy bundle and parting it to reveal that beautiful silver shape inside.

It's a gift to have moments like that to hold on to. Yet a couple of weeks ago, I was taken over to Athol's place for his fortieth wedding anniversary and we got talking about funny things that happen at weddings. I asked him how much he thought Dad's kingfish weighed and he looked at me with a frown and said, 'What kingfish?'

I told him, 'The one he caught the night before he married Catherine. The kingie the Gods gave him for a wedding present. The one we thought was a sea monster.'

'Oh, yes,' he said, with a chuckle. 'That just about summed up the old man. Always late. And to prove it, he went fishing that night, didn't he? When he should've been going out somewhere. Catherine damned near called the whole thing off. It was a case of no fish, and almost no wife too.'

'What do you mean, "No fish"? It was the biggest kingfish I've ever seen,' I said.

'No. That was another time,' Athol insisted. 'He came back empty-handed the night before he got married.'

'We ate the steaks that night and the next morning. And we gave a whole lot away,' I said. 'You can't have forgotten.'

'Yes, but that was a year or so later. We had to go down to the beach and help him land it. He was all in and he wouldn't have managed without us. I'll never forget our fire and the soaking we got.'

There wasn't any point in discussing the matter any further. I was only too well aware that we had avoided chewing over the events of that night, and I had always thought the fault was mine. It had never occurred to me that for some problematical reason Athol might have managed to transpose his memories to a different, safer time.

But I knew I was right. Every detail and every word had been carved into my whole being. So perhaps the only way of looking at Athol's version of what happened is to accept that there is no absolute truth to fishing. Its moments of perfection are all in the mind. If he had chosen to lose the gift of that experience, there was no way of restoring it to him.

Yet it's a pity in a way, because I'm an old man and I had an itch to tell someone at last how that fish had changed my life. Without being able to give my fears a name and deal with them, as Catherine had managed to do the night before she got married, I'd been secretly scared witless by those hours of waiting at the beach. I used to wake up with nightmares about the whole horror for years after. I couldn't come to terms with it. The memory tormented me.

And the experience made an early bird out of me. I've never been able to be late for anything important in my whole life. My children and my grandchildren often call me 'Mr Early'. It's a family joke, with a special private meaning for me.

Everyone seems to laugh at my genius for always being ahead of time. But it isn't the result of strength of mind or self-discipline; it's fear that has made the way I am. Without closing my eyes, I can still see that little clinker-built kauri dinghy rising on the crest of a roller. Helplessly, I watch it hurtle towards me, then my late father, with his oars working frantically, is clutched backwards, to disappear forever into an invisible trough. I couldn't force myself not to be early even if I wanted to.

~ ~ ~

Rivers Without Eels

~

RANGI FAITH

This jack salmon has been in a hungry river
long enough for the scales to float free;
untouched, deep, as rigid as a board
it lies on an angle to the river's flow,
the hooked jaw open,
& the eye a white marble.

There are months, they say, when the eels dig
deep into the mud, months without an 'r',
May and June, July and August,
the winter months that give the river
half a chance,
might live until the next spring.

The gallery is silent—
in the darkness,
two hinaki float in mid-air
suspended on nylon gut;
the air streams past
and filters through the flax;
in the shadows, necks and eyes
slowly rise to the scent
of a fresh current.

Against the far white wall of the gallery
a jet-black eel in a crystal clean aquarium
has given up on the light and movement
and has retreated hard into the curl
of the eel pot's lip,
the bubbles from the pump bursting
on its skin;

in the rivers the winter is biting,
fellow eels are dreaming in the mud.

With the set net cut,
the river flows free,
an elder will sleep easier tonight.

~ ~ ~

Opihi

~

KEN CORLISS

I was with the Purple Grouse and Whisky Dun. Away from salt water Jon was wearing his fly-hat and had become Whisky Dun. The Grouse, of course, wouldn't be seen dead in salt water and was thus always the Grouse.

He was planning our day on the southern river as we drove. Whisky sat in the back of the van, nursing a fragile head. ('The lead poisoning's flared up again'), though I'd noticed it was strangely absent during the previous night's party.

'This is my plan,' announced the Grouse. 'We'll drop you off the bridge'—he was looking at me—'Whisky and I will then go and fish a tributary for a couple of hours. It's fly only so there's no point you coming. You can thrash your way upstream to the next bridge. We'll meet you there and the three of us can have a quick flick for about an hour. We should time it right if you don't muck around. Don't spend 30 minutes in one spot if nothing's happening. Keep moving and cast only in the best possies. Forget about stalking the backwaters or any other water with scum on it. If there's a trout somewhere like that it'd be a bloody miracle and we don't want any part of that.'

'I wouldn't mind one right now,' groaned Whisky.

The Grouse chopped the van down a cog and we slowed as we crossed the bridge. My drop-off point was on the other side. We're sharp-casting buccaneers, I thought, plying the land's water veins and arteries, and plundering the baubles they sheltered. We could throw our lines unerringly and pluck them out, these trout with their dripping fins and their cold eyes, and us with our Sage cutlasses and plans and packed lunches.

'Water looks good,' observed the Grouse.

We all looked between the bridge struts and down to the river below. The water did look good, bubbling green and foamy in the shallows and slow and blue in the pools. Its bed was wide, with 3 or 4 fishable braids running the length of the stretch we could see. Willows trailed their lime-green fronds into the water by the banks and a skilful caster should be able to cover the channels underneath, bobbing a dry down the current just beyond the reach of the submerged willow tips, and hunting down deeper with a bouncing nymph. I could flail it with a twirling Meps.

We parked the van. The Purple Grouse and Whisky Dun quietly picked up their rods. 'Yes, very attractive holding water,' murmured the Grouse. The pair of them quickened their pace, slid down the stony bank and arranged themselves along the better lies of my stretch, flicking their pre-rigged apparatuses with indecent haste and then racing on to the next prime lie. I mucked about with my threadline gear, took my pack from the van and watched them from the road. They rapidly exhausted the pools in the immediate vicinity, the Grouse's crane-fly legs having the edge on the jaded Whisky. They sauntered back with nothing to show for their pre-emptive strike, looking vaguely sheepish, thrusting their shoulders back in an attempt to look bigger and thus more formidable.

'Just checking,' blustered Whisky, tossing his rod in. 'Could still be fish there, we didn't cover it all. Try that little pocket by the log.' He waved his arm briefly in the direction of the horizon. 'See you by the next bridge in a few hours.'

They drove off fast, closely followed by a billow of dust.

I chose the braid that hugged the true right bank and moved upstream, stopping not far from the pylons. A man on horseback wandered in under the bridge from somewhere downstream. The horse lowered its head and its lips nuzzled the surface of the river. I sailed a red Veltic out over a wide pool and watched the horse drinking. The Veltic clunked into the top ring and the horse lifted its head, momentarily streaming a beard of river water. Perhaps that beard held the scent of a trout.

I cast again, splash, in the middle. It landed and drifted downstream and I felt something give it a wee bunt and then hang onto it. Must be weed, I thought, there's no size or fight to it, so I received a prick of adrenaline when I reeled in a trout. A fingerling brown that cavorted like a sprat when I untangled it from the spinner. I held it out to show the horse which snickered in appreciation. The man on the horse smiled. From the distance between us I could have been displaying a coloured pebble, or presenting bloodied stigmata for their inspection. The purple sprat bolted from the palm of my hand when I placed it in the water. I moved a few steps up, as instruction demanded, and cast again. There was a bump on the line as another fingerling threw itself onto the Veltic's barbs and was dragged upstream in open-mouthed confusion when I reeled it in. Across the surface of the pool stipples of more trout appeared as they swirled and skipped about. There's a school of them out there, I thought, all keen for the lure, but it's a bit tough on them chasing the spinning blade and ending up with a jawful of steel for their troubles. They're too small for that nonsense. I'll catch just the one more then leave them to it.

The horse and rider trotted out of the river and departed. I bent my rod tip at them in farewell, cast out and caught the last baby trout, then trotted out of the river like the horse. The Lilliputians could disport themselves without the distraction of my menacing presence.

Following the braid up and around a corner, out of the view of the world, I came across a line of dipping willows. Trunks of trees like monsters skulked below the waterline and created dark places for fish to hide. How could I draw them out from their cold caves?

A shadow detached itself from the bottom of the thin water on my side of the braid and sprang away into one of those dark holes. It wouldn't come out again for a while. I continued walking. Two more shadows lifted themselves up from their resting places and flew across to the deep side. I could walk up here all day and scare every fish in the river. I could tell the Grouse and Whisky that I'd rustled up dozens of fish, but didn't have the heart to catch them. For heart they'd read talent, so at some stage I'd have to have a go at actually landing a big'un.

The islands between the braids were covered in plants, scrubby bushes and spiky flowers mainly, but here and there, where the river had cut little canals across the stones, the cresses had taken over in lush beds. I could lie down here and sleep for hours, the day slipping away and the Grouse and Whisky Dun waiting impatiently up at the bridge.

'He'll be curdling a barren backwater,' they'd say. 'We'll give him 10 minutes then we'll fish the next stretch without him.' And I'd doze on in my blanket of cress and dream of underwater holes and monsters till the sun burned my face and the insects drew blood.

Overhead a flight of ducks whistled by. Strangely, they formed the shape of a fish in the sky. They held the shape till they disappeared from sight. This had to be a good sign. Propitious, Whisky would say.

I sniffed the air like a dog on the quail and began in earnest to seek out a likely haunt.

Further ahead the flow was arrested by an outcrop of limestone the size of a house. The current hit the limestone, had its energy dissipated by the obstruction, then welled backwards into a spreading pond. Deep water built up before managing to slip around the outcrop, gather its forces, and become a river once more. It was a healthy backwater situation right in the middle of the river. It was my cup of tea come home to roost. Ponderous, whirlpooly water that was dangerous and exciting. A hole so deep that it was a hole on the other side of the world. There was a weed bed on one side of it that shelved away steeply.

I switched the Veltic for a Rapala and flung it over the hole onto the wall of limestone. It tinkled down the rock and dropped into the maelstrom below. Down, down it sank before I pulled it back in, attempting to make it swim along the face of the weed bed. It came up from the impenetrable blue, about a foot out from the weed, and dogging it gracefully was the grey shape of a fish. Brobdingnagian in stature! Waggle, waggle went the Rapala, with the trout gliding along behind, then coming in fast for the kill. It was so close now I could make out the rosettes either side of its spine, its colours catching in the sun, and the membranes flexing between the rays of its fins. By narrowing my eyes I could make out its heart beating rapidly under the scales and skin. That's what I reckon anyway. I stopped breathing, messed up the angle of the rod on the retrieve and dragged the lure into the weeds. My big 'un turned on a sixpence and slipped back into the murk. Oh duffer, thy name is me!

But I'd touched the hem of possibility. I dug my feet deeper into the sand, establishing a solid platform for the expected fight, and cast again, once more trailing the lure alongside the weed fringe. And up came the immense fish, this time maintaining a respectable distance from the Rapala, so that when I ran out of water and was forced to stop reeling when it lay a foot from the shore, the trout merely turned aside and melted away into the depths. So I changed the direction of the retrieve and slowed it down considerably. It came up again but I could tell it wasn't interested. It was as though it was seeing the Rapala off its property and didn't care for eating it. How many hundreds, perhaps thousands of times had it done this over the years? Each follow startling the particular angler standing here into thinking he had a chance, each angler thinking that he was the only one with the expertise to bring out this big blimp of a trout. And each holding on to the secret for the future.

When I left the pool I imagined that fish to be mine.

The Purple Grouse had instilled in me the methods of reading the water, fast-tracking the time spent in finding the likely lies. It's easy to spot the dangling fish, the ones that come to the top of deep, clear water and loiter there, hang there like they're balloons on a string, pivoting in the current. And easy to spot a Goliath if it rises right in front of me and lingers on the surface while it inhales a bug. I can't miss fish that do these things. But where the water is ripply or stained or dappled, where it is tumbling or foaming or broken, in this water I am an ignorant blind man.

After walking for 10 minutes from the secret pool that held my secret fish I imagined the river emptied of its water, just lifted up and gone, exposing all the hidey-holes of the fish left on the contours of the riverbed. There'd be 3 small trout lined up in that gut there, off to one side of the ridge that's been swept clean by the current. And a biggie under that dripping log, its sides smeared with mud. Deep holes would hold other trout and the pockets behind rocks in the glides would be occupied. The stirring of silt would betray the presence of others.

I could walk the length of the channels, taking care not to step on a fish, and I'd see where they should lie when the water was back in the riverbed.

But I had to read the water and it was often no more than a guess.

I came to a drop-off that flowed into a hollow in the riverbed. The water was clear on the sloping sides but I couldn't see the bottom out in the middle. Has to be one in there waiting for me to come along, I thought. It's perfect, even the Grouse would lay out a line on this beauty. A fish would be resting on the bottom, right in the centre where I couldn't see, and it would be sifting through all the aquatic odds and sods that had been dislodged upstream and swept over the drop-off to where it waited.

I bobbled the Rapala down the flow and let it sink into the hole before pulling it in slowly. A delicate presentation, I thought, requiring a certain control of movement in order to lend it a natural air. And right smack in the middle, right where I'd imagined it to be, a trout took the lure and began shaking it fiercely. The shot of adrenaline that hit me was intense, loosening my knees to the point where I took an unsteady step towards the river. Best not to fall in, I thought. The rod tilted over so I gripped it tighter and tried to hold it higher, while down below, unseen, the fish did its best to break me. Up and down the pool it thundered, peeling off nylon and drumming, drumming, drumming on the line when I tried to reel.

It came to the top and I managed a look at its beaked head, olive green, and its sharp mouth spitting anger. A fine jack.

I had to have patience, so I maintained just enough pressure to tire him, yet gave him a yard or two when he did the business. Then he jumped, spraying river, and then he jumped again, setting up a spread of ripples like a boulder had been thrown in. In my mind I saw Free Willy breaching. The effort must have done for him because he went all quiet and had calmed down so much that I was able to bring him in closer merely by putting more bend in the rod. He slithered onto the stones, his own weight holding him there. No more breaching for you, big laddie.

I pushed him out onto dry land and he rolled on his side and gave me a dim-eyed stare.

Such an elegant fish, blooming with colour, and for a moment I was tempted to spare him. But he'd had a hard time in my clumsy hands and releasing him may have just prolonged his inevitable death. This one's for an open casket I thought. The potent mix of the day and the moment then hit me and I addressed the fish,

No more will you breach on the long silver river

The Gypsy has come and will sting you and kill you
And what will I do when I want you and need you
I'll stand on your bank and I'll look for your rise
The Gypsy will stand and throw stones at your home
And stare where you were with imperfect eyes.

He didn't react, one way or the other. Might be a deaf one.

I bent to remove the Rapala from his lip instead of despatching him first. Probably a concern about smacking the lure with a rock. As I jiggled the Rapala the trout jerked suddenly in a last-ditch crack at escape, driving two points of the treble through the webbing of my right hand between the thumb and forefinger. It was painful.

I stepped on his back to stop him moving and felt around for a rock. There was a hint of malice in the blow that snuffed him.

So I was attached to the lure and the line and the dead fish, and extraction became a problem as the points were in beyond the barbs. I removed the lure from his mouth and then cut the line, but that was as far as it went: no way could I pull the barbs from the webbing. I decided to leave them hanging there. They hurt each time they moved and they moved a lot. After putting the trout in my pack I went to move on but before I did I walked into the river till the water came to my knees. I bent forward and ducked my head under. The current rushed into my ear and I opened my eyes and looked around. There wasn't much to see, a bed of rounded stones with blurred edges and a snag that I was lucky not to have stuck into my eye. Particles of river debris flowed past. I tried sniffing underwater, hoping to detect a fish upstream but my nose filled with water and I was forced to surface in a coughing fit. Would I or would I not tell the Purple Grouse about my attempt to sniff the fish?

It was very difficult to continue fishing but I persevered despite the pain. Every cast caused the Rapala to pull on the skin and when reeling in it bumped about on every turn of the handle and probed like an attacking wasp. I was a wounded buccaneer battling the odds and the pirates of adversity.

Perhaps I could trail my impaled hand through a likely lie and entice a trout to take the lure. Such honour and awe that would be heaped upon me.

The bridge was in sight when the next strike came. I'd been fishing the last couple of hundred yards left to me, a stretch of river with not enough features to make it interesting. I was rather rushing it too, thinking I'd had my fun for the day and looking ahead to comparing notes with the Grouse and the Dun. Fishing on your own is a licence to embellish.

I was nearly finished with the wide glide, and the hand ornament was playing up. It was pretty much the last trundle of the lure when I got the strike.

The line started jumping off the reel and was pulled over to the far side. Then up and down the current it went as the fish made its confusing runs, and every time I wound the reel the barbs dug a little deeper into my right hand. It was a double hook-up all right, one on each end of the rod. I worked the trout closer to my side and I could make out its shape from time to time when it came to the surface with the line cutting through the water near its head. A shelf of white limestone jutted out from the bank for about 20 feet. The shelf was just under the surface and was like a vast sight board. The trout tired and I got it over the limestone and held it there. It was a hen of probably 3 pounds, giving me the scope to call it 8 when I informed the others after its release.

I wondered why, if I was going to lie about its size, that I even needed to catch it in the first place? Why does anyone? I could merely walk the river without the bother of fishing at all and concoct an entire day's fun. Ten of them, honest. And every man jack of 'em a double figure!

It swayed in the flow, the white background a contrast to its slim outline, and I thought about my next move. I took my right hand off the rod butt to ease the pain in the webbing and the rod tilted forward sharply. The line loosened immediately and I looked over and saw the 12-pound (why not) behemoth sliding across the shelf and dropping out of sight. Gone to run some fresh water over its pricked mouth. It had beaten me fair and square, seizing the chance during my moment of inattention.

I sat down in the scrub for a while and let the sun recharge me.

A pair of terns fluttered downstream, taking the occasional insect in the blinking of an eye. The bones in their wings seemed as fragile as dry twigs and I expected a snap at any time and to see them cartwheeling to the water. Squeak, squeak and they too were gone. The others were waiting for me, lounging on the grass verge beside the road. 'Purple. Whisky,' I greeted them as I approached.

Two large trout lay on the grass beside them.

'You did all right then, I see.'

'Not bad,' said the Grouse. 'The water was a tad low and they were very flighty. One good one each though, for the freezer, and we would've released 4 between us. How about you? Lose your tackle box, did you? I see you keep your Rapalas in your hand now.'

So I had to explain.

'The hooks actually detach from the body of the lure,' said the Grouse. 'Tricky for you, but you could have done it. Would have made life a bit easier. Go and hold your hand in the river for about 10 minutes. The cold water'll make it go numb and I'll whip the barbs out before you have time to faint.'

They busied themselves with coffee and lunch while I squatted down the bank with my hand in the water. Somewhere downstream, the fish that I'd lost was doing the same thing with her mouth.

I believe the Dun would have bought me down a cup of coffee if he'd thought of it.

'Wish I had a beer. My liver thinks my throat's been cut,' I heard him say.

When my skin was suitably anaesthetised the Grouse ripped out the hooks with a pair of angling pliers, leaving only two pinpoints of blood and a slight tear. It was very disappointing, though I did notice a tinge of bruising setting in.

I told them about my catch and my loss.

'Did you have a look at the backwater-type pool in front of the limestone boulder?' asked the Grouse. 'Everybody stops there for a look at old Hulk Hogan. He'll usually come out and tease you, but of course he hasn't got that big by being silly. No, he's a bit of a legend round here, not a show in hell of catching him but he puts on a convincing act for the new chum. Bump into him, did you?'

'. . . uh . . . naturally,' I blustered. 'The Hulk and I go way back. I always stop to check on him—you know, make sure he's in good nick and to admire him. Brought him out a couple of times to have a close look then went about my real business.'

'Never seen him before, have you?'

'. . . no, not really. Never. I thought it was a kind of one-off magic show with an audience of one.'

It wasn't my secret at all. He wasn't my fish. But I think I'd known that all along, and it didn't matter.

'Doesn't matter though,' echoed the Grouse. 'Old Hulk Hogan is everyone's. He's a constant.'

I didn't touch on the subject of ducking my head under. Perhaps if I'd held it there for longer. Maybe 10 minutes. Then I'd have smelled something. Also, I didn't mention the little chat about loss I'd had with the deaf trout. It was of no real consequence to the Grouse or the Dun; it was a personal matter.

While we rested it was decided that we'd fish for no more than an hour on the next section of river and that I would fly fish on a borrowed rod. I picked up one of the Dun's and gave it an exploratory whip or two. It had Orvis Battenkill stamped on the butt. For some reason the Dun started to look uneasy and his arm moved as if to take back the rod.

'This one'll do,' I said, 'Thanks Whisky.'

He relaxed. Whatever his problem was it had gone. He'd been angling for years and was a tolerant man. Unbroken.

'If I can keep lunch down I think I'll come right,' he said. I thought I saw his problem.

We crossed over the road and re-entered the river. Very graciously I was given the first decent pool we came to.

'Fish it up to the eye,' said the Grouse, 'and I mean right up to the eye. This is the best pool you'll get and you've got to make the most of it. Take extra care up by the eye. You've got a Pheasant Tail nymph and a Royal Wulf dry which will also act as an indicator. If the line stops, strike immediately. If the dry bobs under, wait a second or two then strike. We'll wander on ahead and let you go at your own pace. See you soon.'

'Right then.'

I walked into the river, clutching the Orvis, until the cold nipped at my knee-caps. I noticed the Dun glance back over his shoulder as he walked away. He wasn't looking at me, he was looking at the rod.

I lay the line in the water and stripped off more, allowing it to stream down on the current. Okay, I thought, a false cast or so and I'll shoot it right on up there. Tip forward to two o'clock then cock it back to 10 o'clock. Forward to 4 o'clock then back to 8. I was getting the hang of it. The next false cast went forward to 6 o'clock and back to 6 o'clock; a wild, full-blooded, out-of-control flailing of leader and hooks that whacked a thistle on the backcast and then whistled forward like a broken hawser and settled beautifully on the surface of the water about 40 yards upstream. A cracker!

It came back towards me fast and I watched that Wulf corking along like a raft in the rapids. When it was 40 yards behind me I flung the lot up ahead once more. Halfway back it stopped.

I pressed the forefinger of my sore hand tight on the line against the rod and got the loose line onto the reel. There didn't seem to be a great deal of weight on but it was holding against the current. I gave the handle a tentative crank and the resistance on the other end inched closer. It didn't want to run so I lifted the rod tip and kept the pressure steady. After 5 minutes there was still no run so I wound in a few more feet of line.

Maybe the weight was quite solid after all, it was hard to tell, so my strategy became one of maintaining a tight line for some minutes then carefully winding in a couple of turns. It took a lot of concentration, but I didn't want a mess-up. Up ahead, two distant figures were facing my way. They know I've got one on, I thought, let them admire my poise and heed my piscatorial sang-froid. Even the experts can learn, and those two were not so wearied by years of trout contact not to thrill to the sight of my inanimate angling style.

Ten more minutes and two cautious drags later and I noticed they'd gone back to their own fishing. The drama must have drained them.

My charged focus began to falter. A good half hour had gone by since I'd hooked up and still there was no blistering run pulling away from a smoking reel. This trout might be so large it doesn't realise it's hooked. It's just moving forward every now and then when I wind. A fractional inconvenience that it can't fathom.

I turned the handle and walked towards the point at which the line entered the water. Perhaps if the trout saw me it would move. The dry came clear of the water, the fish shouldn't be far behind it. But there was no bulky shape to be seen on the bottom and I was certainly close enough to have noticed had there been one. I slowly drew the rod back over my shoulder, and bouncing along in the shallows I saw a stone. Quite a big stone, about fist-sized, and lodged in a crevice was my scruffy Pheasant Tail. It had taken me 40 minutes to land it.

I squinted at it for a while before I pinched off the nymph. A stone! Perhaps I should hit it with a trout.

Mercifully the other two weren't privy to the denouement, and my embarrassment slowly crawled back into its shell. In fact there was an outside chance I could turn the incident to my advantage, given a speedy hook-up and a little luck. You make your own luck, so it's said, so I must have done something right, because two casts later I was connected again. To a fish. I'd put the nymph and the dry down right alongside the centre current, just below the fabled eye, and the rod tip bent forward and the reel kicked in my hand. Thank heaven for that and let the line hold.

'Still on!' I yelled to the others. I attempted the pose of a man who is slightly bored with the fight yet still in control of it. They turned to look and one of them shouted something that was carried away on the breeze and on the babble of the river. My kiss blown in the dark. Probably encouragement, I thought. They're gee-ing me up.

There was a buffeting of water out in the middle as the trout swished about on the surface. Then it drilled deep and fast and I thought the nylon would give up on me. I followed the run as best I could by scrambling along the bank and taking back line whenever I considered it to be safe. I could feel the fish shaking down there on the bottom, squirming at rope's end.

The Purple Grouse and the Whisky Dun were coming downstream to meet me. So far as they knew I'd been playing the same fish for 45 minutes, a feat of angling surely not met in their ken.

'What are you doing?' said the Dun. 'Leave the poor thing alone, you've been mucking about with it for ages. By the looks it's not exactly a leviathan. You should have beached it by now.'

The Grouse chipped in. 'Its lactics'll be off the register, you can't release it now. It's a taker.'

The noise in my head was the sound of my ruse backfiring, and I was forced to carry through the lie. Ever so calmly I permitted my smugness to be replaced by shame.

'Walk it over that way,' said the Grouse. 'Side-strain it onto that sandy ledge but don't put too much pressure on after it's grounded. I'll nudge it out for you when you get it there.'

I managed to do as he said and with a booted foot he pushed the quite lively body of my trout onto the stones. It was maybe 2 pounds in weight.

'It's got no right to be that lively,' murmured the Grouse.

Despite myself, I felt a prickle of pride. The old dog was on heat again.

I killed the fish as it lay in a puddle.

'Tell you what we'll do with this one,' continued the Grouse, 'When we get home I'll Gyotaku it for you, sort of a memorial for it. It deserves something special after all it's been through.'

Sure does, I thought, considering it took only 5 minutes to land and would have been released had I not decided to grandstand.

'Gyotaku it?' said the Whisky Dun. 'Whatever that is, it doesn't sound legal. Restrain yourself and just eat it.'

'We'll do that afterwards,' explained the Grouse. 'All I'll be doing to it is making a print of it. You dry off one side of the fish then sort of paint the skin with water-colours, trying to match the colour and hue of the trout. You paint in all its spots and fins and tail and head, everything that's on the trout, as best you can. On the one side only, you understand. Then you carefully press a sheet of rice-paper, or something similar, hard down onto it. You can get a beautiful impression of your fish and of course, a record of it. It's Japanese. That's Gyotaku.'

'Oh, right,' I said. 'Yeah, let's do that.'

We did do it later that night and it came out rather well. He had a bit of trouble with the eye and the gill from memory, but he filled them in after he'd made the print. The Gyotaku has been folded and put in a box now. I came across it recently and I noticed I'd written '6 pound' on it. It didn't look that when I caught it and it didn't look it on the print. Sometimes I can't stop myself.

~ ~ ~

Te Puru

(the plug)

~

PITA RIKYS

When the old man returned from hospital he found the valley running from the beach set out in rows of white pegs with bright pink bands painted on them. The pegs, planted alone, sometimes in pairs and occasionally in mysterious clusters, ran from the coast road past the cemetery and the site of the old village and pa, over the ridge and out of his vision to where the motorway looped and growled. The orange glow could be seen at night and the noise of traffic carried in the still night air. The family told him after it was a new interchange to bring traffic from the coast directly onto the motorway. It had been talked about for years. While he didn't understand it fully, it filled him with a sense of niggling disquiet. The route missed the old pa site by fully 20 feet but ran directly over the spot where his aunt's house once stood—the place where he had spent much of his childhood. He knew every tree and bush in the area, every rock, every indentation in the ground; in a way he had grown with them. But he knew much more than that, for his grandfather lived for years with his aunt and he had walked every inch of this land with the old chief many, many times. He could still picture the knotted walking stick his grandfather used, with the scowling dark faces entwined around its length and the blue-green eyes of paua shell, which seemed to him to glow as dusk fell.

His grandfather had taught him, patiently, thickly, in the native tongue, and well. Recounting and reinforcing the stories, legends, myths, prophecies and history of the tribe and the land it was rooted in.

The old karaka tree, half-dead like him, stood in the middle of the interchange area—it was here a century earlier his people had celebrated a famous victory over their foes from the north. On the young limb of that very tree the then chief had hung the breastbone taken from the leader of the attacking war party. On the edge of the interchange area stood a nondescript collection of large boulders. It was among these boulders that his ancestress had hidden from her searching kin until she could elope later in the night with her lover, a handsome young warrior from a neighbouring tribe. And so on . . . Every escarpment, one the site of the first fishing pa centuries earlier, every promontory. The famous kumara gardens renowned throughout the whole area. All gone now. He did not consciously bring them to mind—it seemed as if they had always been part of him.

It didn't matter in one sense, for all the land in the valley had been acquired by the Crown when he was a younger man. All except the cemetery. Only the dead lay in the old ground now. His family group had been one of the last to hold out against the blandishments of the Crown. They stood firm on the old papa kainga. Then the meeting house mysteriously burnt down. The Crown compulsorily acquired the remaining pieces of land and the people were relocated to a nearby hillside—into state rental houses. But all that was in the past.

He had tried to pass on the knowledge his grandfather entrusted to him, but his own children had shown no interest and had left home as soon as they could—mainly to seek work—scattering to the 4 winds. The few mokopunas left in his orbit proved even less interested than his own children; they did not speak the native tongue and preferred television and sport to long walks with an old man who was always stopping to empty his incontinent bladder.

As he grew older it worried him more and more but he found no solution. He thought of writing it down, but he expressed himself poorly on paper, having had little formal education and his memory slowly growing dimmer.

As the families grew in the rental houses on the hill so demand for space became extreme. His wife had died years ago. Most of his close family were driven to move elsewhere. He gave up his house to his niece with a large family, runaway husband and nowhere else to go. With his meagre savings he purchased a small second-hand caravan, which was put on blocks near the spare outhouse in his old backyard. He was nearly self-contained.

Except for one thing that he kept pretty much to himself. That one thing was fishing. He knew more about that small stretch of coast than any other living man. Every morning, unless the weather was very bad, he could be seen with his flax fishing kit and sugar sack under one arm, heading down to the sea.

He knew every type of fish that visited that area, when they visited, the tides, feeding habits and preference, their reaction to different weathers, their spawning cycles, the birds that associated with them. The knowledge had been gleaned from a lifetime of observation, by studying the contents of the stomachs of the fish he caught and noting the patterns. By studying the coastline and allowing for the changes wrought by man and his ideas of progress. He also studied and harvested the shellfish—mussel, from the wharf or a small bed only he had noticed, the ever dwindling pipi from the sand banks by the tide channels and the pupu from the beach at low tide. They acted as food and bait. He didn't always fish, but when he did he never returned empty-handed. He always stopped when he had caught 3 fish of good size—small fish went straight from the line back into the sea.

When he climbed back up the hill he took his bounty to two or three houses in the local community where he knew there was need—pipi one day, fresh fish a day or two later, pupu the next or perhaps puha harvested from the hillside if tide and all else was not in sync. He usually kept some for his niece and her brood and the fish heads he kept for himself. He used to be able to get watercress as well, until the last stream in the area was piped by the council, and consigned underground.

It pleased him to know that he could provide good food for those who needed it most.

By and large he was left to himself, although his niece kept a weather eye on him. The children left him alone—he had no TV in his caravan and they hated the smell from the pot of fish heads slowly cooking. He did not drink or smoke. Listened to the radio sometimes, usually preferred the sound of wind and sea birds—and rest. The few wants he had—mainly clothing, a few sweets and the odd item for the caravan—his niece purchased for him from the pension the government gave him. For years he had been content.

If the weather was warm after he had returned from fishing he could often be found sitting in the sun in an old green armchair, which hadn't changed position in a decade, working on his fishing line.

Years earlier he had tried the nylon lines but developed a distaste for their 'feel', and the first ones were a little brittle, which meant they tangled easily. He made his own lines from flax fibre. The process was very laborious—stripping the leaf, separating the fibre and then slowly knitting it into a line by ribbing and rolling it on the naked thigh. The faded green line, which was the result of many hours of work, was strong and very flexible and almost as invisible to the fish as nylon. Only in one area had he acknowledged modern progress—he used Norwegian steel fish-hooks, Mustads. He kept a life's supply in oilcloth in a tobacco tin in his fishing kit.

That was his life.

When he returned from hospital he knew he was dying. It did not perturb him at all and he accepted it in the same way as he accepted changes in the tide or weather. He had prepared for his death long before now. He slipped back into his old rituals as if nothing had changed. What pain found him, he hid from observation.

But the hospital told his niece, 'It was only a matter of time.' She had asked him if he wanted to be buried or cremated. He joked with her, knowing that the papers in the caravan dealt with that.

'Perhaps I should be buried at sea,' he had responded in the native tongue. 'Give the fishes a chance to have a bite at me,' he continued. 'After all, I have had enough bites of them,' he chuckled.

'In your case,' she replied in English, 'they would only eat the head and spit the rest out.' A relaxed reference to his penchant for fish heads. She left him dozing in the sun.

The next day the conditions were perfect for rock fishing—the day was overcast. With some difficulty he made his way down to a favourite rock shelf nudged into the incoming tide. He felt a little strange. It wasn't until he had finished cleaning his 3 fish and packed them in the sack that he realised his time was near. He noticed a boy from the settlement walking along the coast road, heading home. He waved to him. He gave the boy the sack and kit with instructions to give them to his niece. If she wasn't at home he was to leave them in the kitchen.

If his niece was distracted and did not realise the significance of his actions the incoming tide would eventually carry him off the rock shelf and up the harbour. When it turned it would carry him one last time past his old home and out through the heads to the deep water.

Slowly he sat back—leaning against the slightly warm rock wall—and, pulling his cap down a little to cut the glare from the water, closed his eyes.

~ ~ ~

Fishing with the Colonel

~

DAVID ELWORTHY

I started fishing for trout at the age of 8, with a greenheart rod and a small brass reel that my father had used as a child, one of his cast-off lines which needed constant greasing to stay afloat. He let me use his cat and gut casts that had to be soaked for 10 minutes before use, and I used my pocket money to buy #16 Greenwell's Glories, Heckham Peckhams, and Red-tipped Governors from England McCrae in Timaru.

My father taught me the basics, particularly that long pause so essential for good casting, but it took a long time to get to know our lovely river, which meandered for 3 or 4 miles along the eastern perimeter of the farm. In the late 1940s and early 1950s the trout were there in extraordinary numbers, but I needed to know where they liked to lie and when they liked to feed. I watched the way they moved and the extraordinary variety of hatches as the summer progressed. I don't recall catching even the smallest tiddler until I was tewn, but after that the Little Pareora became my river. We understood one another and the trout responded. I began to try my mother's patience by returning day after day with several trout in my smelly old fishing bag.

Just after Christmas 1947 the rhythm of our summer days on the farm was disrupted by the arrival of an old Dunedin friend of my mother's—Aunt Elizabeth, we were told to call her—and her new husband Colonel John Ewart-Cuthbertson, who was recently demobbed from the King's Own Gurkha Rifles. He had spent 3 years as a prisoner of war in Changi.

Aunt Elizabeth was small and dark, with expressive hands and a quick wit. The colonel—'Just call him Uncle John,' said Aunt Elizabeth—was tall and handsome, with a luxurious black moustache. He was still thin after his wartime ordeal, but he was straight-backed and elegant, and unlike Dad's farmer friends appeared utterly at ease in the drawing room. They were looking at settling in New Zealand, so my mother had said, 'Come and stay for as long as you like.' They arrived with 4 big trunks and occupied the largest guest bedroom for the best part of a year.

We kids had never met anyone like John Ewart-Cuthbertson. From the start he asked us to perform all sorts of tasks for him, such as grooming his horse and polishing his boots. He was a bit scary, so we—my two sisters and two brothers and I—never complained very much. On the second night of their stay Mum and Dad held a party for them, so we were told to stay upstairs. We sat on the landing and although we couldn't see anything we could hear the grown-ups downstairs getting noisier and noisier. We scrambled for our beds when we heard someone come up the stairs. It was the colonel, smelling strongly of whisky. He was fully arrayed in his dress blues, and looked as if he had stepped straight out of one of those elegant cartoons in the old bound copies of *Punch* in the library downstairs. He sat on the side of my brother Jonny's bed and began to tell us stories about life on the North-west frontier.

'Let me tell you about my Gurkhas,' he said. 'They're the most wonderful people in the world. They're so courageous and loyal. They'll never forget me and I'll never forget them.'

The colonel got up, stretched his long legs, and left the room without a word. A minute later he returned, carrying a razor-sharp Nepalese kukri, with his name embossed on its silver handle. He passed it around—all 5 of us were now in Jonny's bedroom. 'I have two favourite languages,' he said, 'and neither of them is English. Hindustani is the most expressive language in the world, and Pushtu the best language for lovers.'

The colonel suddenly crouched down in front of us, his eyes glinting in the dim light from the landing. He really was scary. 'Had a bit of a problem in '37,' he said, swishing the sharp curved blade of the kukri through the air. 'Bloody Pathans invaded our camp after midnight, they caught us by surprise. Gentle chap, my subadar-major, but my God he moved fast. The Pathan lunged at him with his dagger'—here the colonel stabbed the kukri towards the wardrobe, and 10 bony knees rose up sharply—'but Jimche was too fast for him. He leapt to one side and then swung at him with his kukri.'

The colonel stood straight, assuming the stance of the Pathan tribesman.

'"Ha," he sneered. "You missed!"

'"Oh no I didn't," replied the subadar-major. "Just try shaking your head."'

It took us a moment, and then we all roared. So the colonel told us the same story in Pushtu, flopping his head realistically at the punchline, before heading back downstairs.

The following day was clear and beautiful. 'David,' my father called to me as he set out with my brothers to draft ewes in the yards on top of the hill. 'Ask the colonel if he'd like to go fishing. Put him in the best water and make sure he catches something. And for God's sake don't fish in front of him, even in a separate pool. Stay behind.'

'Okay, Dad.'

'Would you like to come fishing, Uncle John?' I asked when the colonel came downstairs.

'Please call me Colonel Ewart-Cuthbertson,' he replied stiffly, but then relented.'Yes, I'd like to do some fishing—haven't cast a fly since '36 in Kashmir.'

'You could borrow some of Dad's gear,' I suggested.

'For goodness sake, boy. I do have my own. I'll show it to you shortly.'

Before long we were sitting eating scones and sunning ourselves on the nursery verandah. The magpies were calling and Mum and Aunt Elizabeth were admiring the roses.

'What are those squawking black and white birds called?' asked the colonel.

'Magpies.'

'They're not magpies. Magpies have long tails. They're pied crows.'

We ate our buttered scones in silence.

'What's that palm tree called?'

'That's a cabbage tree. It's the biggest lily in the world.' I was proud of that information, having recently gleaned it from the *Junior Digest*.

'It's ugly. It's foreign. It should be cut down. Palm trees belong in India, not in this garden.'

'Come and look at my gear,' he barked abruptly.

Two splendid Hardy split cane rods, 4 brand-new Hardy reels and a mouth-watering display of English dry flies—the colonel's fishing tackle was impressive, even to my 11-year-old eyes. He had rubber thigh waders, a tweed Sherlock Holmes cap covered in gaudy salmon streamers, and a wonderful woollen fishing waistcoat, with numerous pockets containing flies, scissors, miniature scales, packets of catgut, a bottle of fly float, a tin of line grease, a tiny whisky flask, a metal cigar container and even a little torch. I was awestruck.

'Uncle John,' I cried, 'you must be the best fisherman in the world!'

'Colonel Ewart-Cuthbertson,' he reminded me. 'I'll have a nap after lunch. After that I shall take you fishing.'

When we walked down the road to the river in the late afternoon the colonel was wearing his rubber waders, his fishing waistcoat, a tweed jacket and his Sherlock Holmes cap. Over his shoulder hung a neat little basket—a creel, according to the colonel—already packed with fresh green grass to cradle his catch, and he was carrying two rods. I was travelling rather lighter: khaki short-sleeved shirt, khaki shorts and sandshoes, carrying one rod, one line, one cast and two flies in the little flybox given to me by my grandfather on my tenth birthday.

A light northerly was touching the willows and the river was looking perfect. There had been a good fresh during the previous week but the river was now clear, with lovely little rapids at the head of each pool and almost no sign of weed. We looked down as we crossed the road bridge and saw 4 or 5 small fish rush for cover at the first sign of our shadows. 'By Jove,' said the colonel. 'That looks promising.'

I chose to fish upstream from the bridge, where the river was lined with willows, but where the good pools were more accessible and there were fewer barbed wire fences to pierce the colonel's waders. 'No problem with willows,' the colonel told me. 'I learnt to deal with them on the Test.'

It took a while for us to set up. First our cat gut casts were placed under stones in the water to soften and then the colonel took some time to decide what rod to use, what reel, what line and what fly. Half an hour later he was ready, with a Hardy's Favourite tied to the end of his carefully knotted tippet.

The pool before us ran swift and deep beneath a small cliff, with a steep rapid at its head.

'Look, Uncle John,' I whispered. 'There at the tail of the pool—just near that big white stone.' It wasn't a big fish, but takeable. 'Put your fly just in front of it!'

'Quiet, boy! I know how to fish. Where is it?'

The colonel's first cast landed heavily against the cliff. Miraculously the trout remained undisturbed.

'You're fooling me, lad. There're no fish there.'

'Yes! See him! He's moved to the right of the white stone. See where I'm pointing!'

The colonel's next cast caught a willow behind him, so high that even his tall figure could not reach it. So he snapped the tippet, knotted on a new one and changed his fly. 'No fish there,' he stated. 'I'll try the ripple at the head of the pool.'

He stalked ahead and my first cast behind him was a lucky one. The trout moved across the white stone and sucked down my Red-tipped Governor. As soon as I set the hook it caused a visible bow wave as it sped past the startled colonel towards the head of the pool.

'Hey! I'll have to teach you some angling manners, my boy,' he bellowed. 'It's not done to take my water, you know!'

'Sorry—but I was fishing below you,' I shouted as I tried to entice the trout, a fat little fellow of about 1½ pounds, back to the tail of the pool.

'You've still spoiled the best water,' he replied. 'How can I fish the head of the pool now? I'm going up to the next pool and don't you follow.'

I watched him as he crossed the head of the rapid above, making towards a lovely open pool that always held fish. 'Oh well,' I thought as I landed the trout, banged him on the head and placed it in my bag. 'No harm in having a bit of a go at the head of this pool now that he's left it.'

Two of my next 4 casts were lucky and I picked up a couple more fish, one larger and one slightly smaller than the first one. The colonel, who appeared to be untangling his line at the head of the next pool, failed to notice the action downstream.

He was sweating when I caught up to him. 'Lost two barbs,' he said. 'Can't understand it. Now let's look at that fish. It should have been mine, you know. In England or Kashmir you'd be shot at dawn if you pinched another man's water like that. Good gracious—3 of them! Big ones, and all in my water!'

'Sorry, Uncle John.'

'Colonel Ewart-Cuthbertson to you, young man, and don't you forget it!'

I waited well back while the colonel once more moved straight to the rapid at the next pool's head. He overcast on his first two attempts, perhaps misjudging the strength of the light breeze behind him, but the next few casts hit the water. He was unlucky not to hook a fish, as I spotted at least 6 at the foot of the rapid after he had given up and moved on up to Peter's Head, a very deep pool which was our favourite summer swimming hole. There was a low willow bough hanging over the water, from which we could jump and dive into the cool deep water.

'Not much going at the tail of this pool, Colonel Ewart-Cuthbertson,' I said. 'But last week I saw a couple of really good ones at the head. Look! There's a rise just below the rapid.'

'Keep well out of my way,' said the colonel as he began to false cast across the stream. His final backcast did flick the stones to my right, but this time the barb obviously survived, for on its way forward it embedded itself in the low willow branch above the stream.

'Bugger,' said the colonel.

'I'll climb out and free it,' I offered.

'No. I don't want the fish disturbed. I'll do it.'

For someone as old as the colonel—he must have been pushing 40—he moved quietly and stealthily as he crossed the tail of the pool, clambered up the opposite bank and climbed the tree, inching slowly along the bough to retrieve his fly. But I should have realised that this was a branch designed for kids, not for tall grown-ups—especially grown-ups who were carrying an extra 50 pounds of assorted fishing gear and thick woollen clothing. The branch cracked and the colonel seemed to fall very slowly into the water with scarcely a splash. The air in his waders forced his feet straight up into the air, but the current drew his struggling figure into shallow water before he could be in any danger of drowning.

I retrieved his sodden cap as it sped down the rapid below then rushed back to help him to his feet. He remained surprisingly quiet, although the colour of his face made me feel uneasy. 'Why don't you take off those wet clothes, Uncle . . . They should dry pretty fast on those stones.'

I helped to pull off and drain his waders and then stood there awkwardly as he sat and reached for his cigars, which were sopping wet, as were his matches. 'Christ,' he said, 'what a bloody country. Look, I'll just sit here for a while. You go fishing.'

So off I went upstream. When I returned half an hour later with a couple more fish in my bag, he was still sitting on the same rock in his clothes, but he was looking a little warmer and drier. He held his little silver whisky flask in his right hand. The sun was just starting to disappear behind the hills to the west, so it was time to head home and find him a hot bath. He struggled again into his wet waders and we started walking downstream.

The colonel remained silent for a while, then he said, 'Catch any more?'

'A couple.'

'Let's look.'

I opened up my bag. The last two trout were both above 2 pounds. We trudged on, the colonel's waders squelching rhythmically at each step. His Sherlock Holmes hat dripped at both ends and his normally swept back black hair was plastered against his forehead.

'David, you can call me Uncle John if you like.'

'Okay, Uncle John.'

'Oh, and David. No need to mention my falling in, you know.'

'But Uncle John, they'll notice that you're all wet!'

'Ah. Tell you what. You could say that I fell in while playing a fish.'

'Okay, Uncle John.'

Another long pause. 'David, I noticed your old reel and line. What if I gave you one of my Hardy reels?'

'Oh Uncle John, that would be fantastic, but I couldn't really take it.'

'Of course you could. I've got another 3.'

'Oh thank you, Uncle John.' I said, wildly excited.

It was cool by now, and we hurried over the bridge before climbing the road towards the house. Uncle John was starting to shiver.

'David, what say I caught 3 fish and you caught two?'

'Oh, you mean. . . oh. Okay, Uncle John.'

Nothing more was said. After a hot bath and a couple of stiff whiskies Uncle John staged a remarkable recovery. 'That was a great afternoon's fishing, Harold,' he said to my father. 'Cunning, lively buggers, your Pareora trout. Playing that

2-pounder made it almost worth while falling in. David's clearly the young fisherman in this family, so I think I'll take him out again next time.'

The colonel insisted on my accompanying him on every fishing excursion until the end of the holidays. He did catch one trout, on his own, on the last day before we returned to school. We celebrated his triumph quietly on the river bank. He gave me a sip of whisky from his flask. It tasted horrible.

After I returned to boarding school he decided to give angling a miss for a while and took up horse riding instead. For my part I was the envy of all my schoolmates when I showed them my beautiful new Hardy reel, not to mention the colourful English flies he had given me each time we caught a fish.

Uncle John eventually decided that New Zealand was not for him, and left the farm just before the next summer holidays began. He took Aunt Elizabeth back to Britain, where they settled in a Hampshire village surrounded by ex-military types just like him. I visited him there once, in 1956. He was much plumper then and looked contented. I wanted to talk to Aunt Elizabeth, but he insisted on taking me on a tour of his wardrobe, which took over half an hour.

A couple of years later a mate and I, carrying heavy packs, were making our way down Piccadilly towards the underground, on our way to Victoria Station and France, when we bumped into the colonel emerging from Burlington Arcade. He was wearing an immaculate pin-stripe suit with a yellow rose in his buttonhole. 'Hello, Uncle John,' I cried. 'How are you?' But he appeared not to recognise me in my checked bush shirt and jeans, and swept on down the street.

Uncle John is dead now. I'm still using the reel he gave me and caught a fish on it only last week. It's just as good as new.

~ ~ ~

Early Days Ashore

~

NOEL BATY

Almost as far back as I can remember I've had a wish to go fishing. I used to watch the trout in the Avon River in Christchurch when I was quite young but there didn't seem to be any way I could go about catching them.

I'd have been about 12 years of age when the family bought a bach at Governors Bay in Lyttelton Harbour. The shoreline had a number of small coves and our bach was in one of them. At each end of the cove was a rocky headland which effectively isolated us when the tide was in. We had to time our visits to catch the lower end of the tides. If by chance we missed the tide, the driver of the service car would drop us off at a place above the bach and we'd slither and slide down a steepish slope to the last small dip onto the beach behind the bach.

This was in 1927 and like so many other families of that time we weren't lucky enough to own a car—unheard of these days. Being without our own transport, we travelled on the service car that ran the Christchurch-Governors Bay route, which met our needs pretty well, as the service was fairly regular, and the drivers co-operative.

Along with the bach we had a rowing boat—a massive craft some 5 metres long and about 1.5 metres in beam, flat-bottomed with provision for 4 rowers.

It was in that boat that Dad and I first went fishing, and I can remember the fine sunny morning clearly. Dad rowed out about 100 metres from the shore and we dropped the anchor. No rods in those days, though I'd rather hankered after one when I'd read about that fellow Zane Grey.

Our tackle was simple—a cotton handline, two or three small cod hooks on catgut traces, and a tin of mussels for bait. We were ready for action. I don't think Dad had done much fishing before, though he was an experienced yachtsman. However he was willing to encourage me because he knew of my keen interest.

We sat there out on the harbour for some time before we began to catch small dogfish and blowfish, but nothing edible came along. That is until Dad told me to hang on to his line while he stoked up his pipe. As soon as I took the line I could feel a fish on the end. Dad wouldn't take the line back. He told me it was my fish and to go ahead and get it in. It was a large red cod—my very first fish and a beauty! As soon as it hit the bottom of the boat it regurgitated its last meal which happened to be a number of small flounder each about the size of a large postage stamp.

We used the best of them for bait and in no time we were pulling in cod two at a time until we had enough to feed the family for a couple of meals. I think we could have just about filled the fish box, but there wasn't any point in catching fish we couldn't store. No fridges in those days.

The run of cod lasted a couple of days and each morning soon after sunrise Dad and I would be on the water. I think he was beginning to get interested in fishing too. I also believe he wanted to get me keen on boating because after a stint of rowing with one oar alongside him, he let me take the two bow oars which were shorter and more manageable for my strength at that age. Subsequently he let me do all the rowing unless the wind got up. Then we'd use two oars each and, after some pretty erratic manoeuvres, we got into some sort of rhythm and got along quite well—apart from a few crabs I caught from time to time which ended up on my back in the bottom of the boat.

A rocky outcrop at the left of the cove offered a challenge for a budding angler. The water was deep and green, but the long arms of kelp stopped me from using my handline there, although something told me there had to be fish there.

When I saw the bamboo windbreak growing on a nearby property a solution seemed obvious. Zane Grey used a rod, didn't he, though he had a reel to hold the line. Well, first the rod. The farmer let me take a bamboo pole about 4 metres long. I trimmed it up and tied a length of my herring line (the same length as the rod) to the end. A couple of small hooks on catgut traces, a leadhead nail for a sinker and down I went to the water.

It had been a lucky guess. There *were* fish under the kelp. Large guffies—we call them spotties in the North Island—were there in number. Guffies which weighed under a kilo each but which tasted delicious when filleted carefully to avoid the bones.

There were also garfish—or piper if you live in the North Island—and they were also rather bigger than I've seen in the north, and they too were delicious to eat.

One morning a big fish took my bait, but the knot at the end of the rod gave way and I lost the lot. I took more care next time—and I guess that's how we learn by our mistakes.

Another morning a visitor was out in the boat and hooked a large ling. It looked like a big orange-coloured conger eel and proved to be a powerful brute. It thrashed around in the water and the line cut the visitor's hands quite badly before he laid it out with a rowlock.

There was a strange story attached to the little cove. Occasionally we would hear children calling and laughing, but there was never a soul to be seen. One of my brothers-in-law was of enquiring mind, and researched the history of the place. He came back with the sad tale of a massacre that had taken place there before the Pakeha came to New Zealand. The men of a small sub-tribe which occupied the little bay were away when a marauding war party swooped on the women and children, killing them all. It was said the children were laughing and playing together when the war party struck them down, and the sounds we heard were the spirits of the children who died that day.

A less romantic theory put forward was that light winds coming down the harbour carried voices from a playground further round, and the cliffs behind the bach acted as a sounding board. The legend was the sadder version but, in spite of that, we rather preferred it to the more prosaic one.

The bach was sold and another built at Stewarts Gully on the banks of the Waimakariri. That was closer to home and generally more suitable for the whole family, including my sisters and their children. Dad had bought a home on the banks of the Wairarapa Stream which meandered through Christchurch and, as a dedicated and meticulous gardener, he didn't go to the gully very much for a start. He cultivated a magnificent asparagus bed which became his pride and joy. It also became the happy hunting ground for worms.

The little stream held a population of small brown trout. Many were around 500 grams in weight but a few I saw were larger. In fact one that I tried for, without success, finally fell to one of Dad's asparagus bed worms. He weighed more than 1 kilo and was in prime condition.

With the move to the Gully and the availability of those little trout, my interest switched to trout fishing. Worms were permitted for schoolchildren, and as I had nobody to coach me in the art of fly fishing, worms it had to be.

Although the depression was striking everyone and was beginning to hurt us, Dad managed to help me buy a rather cumbersome tubular steel rod. It was 2.7 metres long and had all the action of a wet tea towel. However, it did lob my worms far enough to keep a steady stream of trout appearing on our dinner table.

My Dad died just before World War II started, and the home on the Wairarapa Stream was sold. I moved into barracks at Wigram, so sadly my fishing was put on hold for some years.

～ ～ ～

Eel Fishing

~

JAMES K. BAXTER

Sunlight and floating seeds
On the black surface of the water hole
At the river's elbow, where great eels
Bask on a mud bottom,
And manuka branches from the high bank
Roof the river over.

All at once among the rushes
Two boys come running, splashing,
With bare feet and old clothes,
With eyes brighter than a bird's,
With catgut, hooks, and line,
With quick shouts and silence.
They climb to a branch of the oldest tree
And drop their lines into the bog-black water.

~ ~ ~

Viscount Grey

~

NEVILLE BENNETT

The dry fly must seem natural 'in appearance, position and motion. The fly must float as if it were buoyant, cheerful and in the best of spirits, natural flies having the appearance of being very frivolous and light-hearted.' The writer of those poetic words was Viscount Grey, who became the longest serving, and arguably the best, foreign secretary England ever had. His book, *Fly Fishing*, first published in 1899, became an instant classic. It added a distinct tone of literary elegance to the thousands of prosaic manuals of instruction which angling has generated.

Fly Fishing is a superlative introduction to our noble sport. It covers chalk stream, wet fly for trout and sea-trout, and salmon. In dry fly, he sufficiently wrote, there are 3 objects: 'the first is to rise the trout, the second to hook it and the third to land it'. 'The effort is to make the trout notice the fly without noticing anything else. It is in this that the fine art of any fly fishing consists.' He then proceeded to advise on concealment, casting, striking and playing the fish. His advice is still relevant today. 'It is better to float the wrong fly really well then to bungle with the right one.'

One remarkable feature was Grey's use of only 4 patterns. He used the Olive Quill Gnat in June and the Red Quill in July. If these failed, he might change to a different size of the same pattern, or switch to an Iron Blue, or a plain Black Hackle (Spider).

Despite his lucid prose, Grey is now almost unknown as an angler and writer. Who was he? What did he write? What was his angling experience? The answers to such questions reveal a fascinating man.

Until he was in his thirties, the Gods seemed to smile on Edward Grey. He came from a distinguished family which nutured very liberal politics with a high sense of duty. Grey's forebears made their mark as generals and prime ministers. The family was not rich. Even when Grey was an eminent parliamentarian and company director, he had to rent out each summer his ancestral home, Fallodon. Fallodon is in Northumberland, on the Scottish border, near the small town of Alnwich. As a child, Edward Grey spent hours catching small trout, eels, and flounders, in local brooks.

At school he excelled in angling. He boarded at Winchester, on the Itchen, the world famous chalk stream. Grey taught himself how to catch the highly educated trout in the town. He abandoned the familiar northern wet fly, and learned that success comes only from patience and hard work: that is ' taking the pains and trouble to acquire skill'. He caught one trout in his first year, 13 in the second and 76 in the fourth.

Having mastered the skills, he went to a higher stage of caring for skill more for its own sake and less for the results it brought. Grey teaches us to be content when the first hour's angling is fruitless, if we are doing things well and skilfully and thereby deserve success.

He did not show the same determination in academic matters. He entered Balliol College, Oxford, but was expelled for idleness. He must have been remarkably idle, given Oxford's tolerance of well-connected aristocrats. Grey almost immediately entered Parliament. He was a champion of the rural working class and held his seat for more than 30 years. Loyalty to his constituency prolonged Grey's political career, for at later elections he had 'the coward hope that defeat would set him free'. Grey was made Under-Secretary for Foreign Affairs upon election. Perhaps his contemporaries were awed by his brilliant public speaking—he outshone Churchill and Lloyd George in a later Cabinet.

Being based in London was a sacrifice, so Grey and his wife Dorothy, who also fished, found a cottage on the Itchen for a weekend retreat. Grey had immense social opportunities, but disregarded most invitations and left London hurriedly on Friday afternoons, or very early on Saturdays, to fish. It was not good form to fish on Sundays, so then he pursued his equally important hobby of bird watching. He did accept invitations to visit Kind Edward at Balmoral—as long as it was salmon season! Life at the cottage was bliss. There Grey wrote *Fly Fishing* and in 1905, *The Cottage Book*.

But in 1905 Grey's life disintegrated. Until then this handsome man had the world at his feet: superb fisherman, businessman, and eminent politician. Then Dorothy died. Grey became Foreign Secretary 1906-16. He served in an innovative Cabinet much beset by policy differences and later, war. Grey was exhausted by politics.'I do long to be in the country—without having to work early before I go out, and late after I come in.'He later said,'I was always really miserable and out of place in politics.'

He became a tragic figure. Bereft by his wife's death and the deaths of two brothers, distraught by the lack of sons—the Greys died out—and by the fires that destroyed his family home and the cottage, he then faced blindness which ended his work and ruined his recreation. His diary for May 29, 1917 reads,'The Itchen trout are more fat than I have seen them for many years. I landed a beauty of 2lb and 3oz and 5 other fish. I am much handicapped as I cannot see my fly on the water and if there is any wind . . . I cannot tell where the fly is. The relief of being out of office continues to be unspeakable.' Soon his eyes deteriorated further and his Braille finger failed too.

In better times Grey's calendar involved a variety of fishing. From March to May he fished with fly for salmon in Scotland. He considered it '. . . one of the great moments in the joy of life', when a bite came. He asserts the need to be keen and alert through hours of unrewarding casting, and gives examples of days that began slowly but produced fish of 30 pounds. Recalled by Cabinet urgently, he once caught 8 huge salmon in a stolen hour's delay.

In May, June and July he fished the chalk stream. In August and September he went north to Fallodon, to the Highlands, or more rarely, Ireland. On these expeditions he varied his quarry, but enjoyed catching sea trout.

Grey's only vanity was to fish dry when others fished wet. One day he angered the northern locals by catching 31 fish while they drew blanks. 'Dry fly', they snorted. 'We know nothing about dry fly here.'

There is in Grey's writing an elusive moral dimension. He reminds us that fishing requires hard work and continual effort, that the angler needs the quickness of limb, accuracy of eye, and strength, necessary for success in more competitive games. The angler also needs self-control, especially in the biter disappointment of losing a fish. He impresses with his treatment of the natural world. When strained by overwork we are, he says, '. . . out of tune and cannot expect good sport.'

Grey said also, 'Like friendship, in Nature we cannot take all and bring nothing.'

~ ~ ~

A Bum Steer

~

OWEN MARSHALL

I wear a pair of thigh waders when I clean the car. My wife laughs at me because, she says, I look a fool. My sons snigger too, as they slouch past with adolescent élan. The waders are old, and the rubber has frayed away in the crease lines, but they do the trick for me when I'm using the hose on the car. It's annoying to get your feet wet at such a chore.

For years the waders have been used only at home, but there was a time when I did a good deal of trout fishing—not salmon fishing, because I always found that too competitive, too crowded. I fished as much to be alone in the countryside as anything else, and jostling almost shoulder to shoulder with others after salmon at a river mouth didn't do much for me.

I bought the waders in the year that I shifted to Oamaru to be information officer at the council. 'You'll have to get decent waders of course,' said Ted. Ted Mumsome was my immediate boss, and a very keen fisherman. In the season most of each Monday's morning tea break was filled with Ted's monologue of his fishing exploits over the weekend: the relative merits of Grey Ghost, or Yellow Dorothy, until his colleagues were driven back to their desks. In retrospect at least, these excursions showed Ted to be a sort of Bwana of the waterways, replete with knowledge and expertise to outwit the most wily of trout and fellow anglers.

Once he knew that I fished a bit, Ted decided to take my education in hand and, given his seniority and possible effect on my career, I went along with it. One of Ted's rather irritating habits was that he was a contradictory conversationalist: one of those people constitutionally inclined to propose the opposite of anything you suggest. If you said the day looked promising, he was full of dire prognostication. If you praised someone for affability, or talent, Ted gave a rueful laugh and said you didn't know the half of it. Any suggestion concerning timing, or venue, of any activity whatsoever, was met by Ted's determined alternative. To express any view at all was the preamble of inevitable debate. It got rather wearying, and was probably the reason that Ted didn't have many friends among the council staff. Anyway, he realised that as I was a new chum of no great status, he could be the chief to my Indian, and I found it politic to go along, at least at first.

The Waitaki is a big river, but I never found it as good for trout as I expected. The main channels were a great deal swifter than I was used to. Ted took me out 4 or 5 times that first year, and I tried to escape his persistent instruction and criticism by going off down a bank by myself as much as I could. Then, late in the season, on a long, warm, still North Otago evening, we drove up from Oamaru on what was to be our last fishing trip together. There was a sign at the Glenavy camping ground which said 'Fish In River Now', and most of them would stay there ·it seemed to me.

'So what spot do you reckon would be best on a day like this?' asked Ted.

'Maybe the old crossing?' I said.

'Hopeless. Absolutely hopeless. The stone wall is the place to go today. There's more trees and we want shadow on the water.'

'Right,' I agreed.

We drove up the north side of the valley and pulled off to park by the stone wall. As we stood by the car boot, putting on our waders and getting our gear sorted, Ted gave me a lecture on where the fish lie when there's broken water. He had expensive, green, one-piece waist-high waders, and a flap cap on which he carried most of his flies. He looked a bit of a pillock actually, but I wasn't going to tell him so to his face. Job security was an important part of my philosophy in those days.

'Should we go upstream, do you think?' I asked him.

'No. There's better water below.'

'Maybe I'll just mosey up there a bit and then come on back towards you,' I said. I put up a carefully calculated resistance from time to time so that I didn't lose my self-respect entirely.

'You'll learn the hard way, but suit yourself,' said Ted. 'Don't come crunching into the top of any water I'm fishing.'

We walked together across the greywacke stones, the scattered bleached grasses and docks, through the patches of lupins and broom and gorse. The sun burnt fiercely as if to deny that it must fall down soon. Ted and I parted at one of the channels, and I tried not to seem eager as I turned away from him and went upstream. 'Good luck,' I said. 'See you later.'

'Luck's got nothing to do with it,' said Ted. 'You remember what I told you last time about not moving about too much in the water.' He clumped off down-stream. The waist-high waders accentuated his almost womanly hips, and his shoulders were stooped from desk work. He had a high, arched nose and the bone and cartilage whitened the skin as if to split it at any moment. I wondered what he thought about when he was fishing alone.

Autumn is almost always drought time in North Otago, and the side channels of the Waitaki in particular showed on the stones algae lines of successively lower levels. They weren't letting a lot out of the dams. I headed for a turn of still water, with a small cascade at the top end, hoping there'd be a fish or two there waiting just below the broken water.

I was only a threadline fisherman and never aspired to the almost holy realm of the dry fly. I had one strike at the top of the pool below the rapids, but the medium-sized fish flipped into the air free of the lure, and after that I never even saw a rise. I worked down the reach quietly, looking and casting unhurriedly. Much of the time I just stood there, enjoying the cool of the back channel through my waders, and watching the sun go slowly down. A long arrow of Canada geese went up the valley, and their honking echoed in the evening air. I saw the momentary, syrup strip of a weasel over a pale clay bank; gone before its recognition. Magpies were quarrelling somewhere beyond my sight, and the air was a rich mixture of country fragrances.

Then I heard Ted coming from downstream, marching with slow deliberation among the vegetation. 'You said you were going to work your way down to me,' he said, as if I'd left him stranded at a city bus-stop.

'I was just about to.'

'Well, you're the loser.' Ted held up a resigned-looking rainbow of 2½ pounds or so. 'I could've given you a few tips if you'd been with me. There's no substitute for experience, you know.'

'I guess you're right,' I said.

Ted made himself comfortable on a small bank and investigated the guts of his fish for my benefit, asking me to identify the various items of the fish's recent diet, and contradicting each of my answers. Ted did a post mortem on every fish he caught, and recorded the results in a notebook along with the details of the weather and water conditions at the time of the catch. 'Knowledge is power, you see,' he said. 'That's the same in business as it is in fishing. What's the use of anything if you don't learn from your experience? Eh?' He was right no doubt, but I've always been perverse in not wishing to analyse my recreations.

'Anyway,' said Ted, 'let's take a last half hour or so downstream a bit. I saw a likely place with a bit of depth.' He washed out his fish, wrapped it in newspaper and put it in his bag. 'Move yourself then,' he said, although I was standing waiting for him.

We scrambled up the small bank and made our way through the long grass and longer shadows of gorse and broom of the island flat. A commotion began in the bushes towards the main river. We had just time to see a thrashing line of broom and lupin tops heading our way, before a large Hereford steer burst out a few metres from us and stood glaring, with snot and saliva gleaming in the last of the setting sun. I'm not easy with big animals, and that Hereford was an impressive brute with horns. Anything with horns, from the devil down, deserved respect as far as I was concerned. I backed up and stumbled, to end ignominiously on my back amid the gorse and bleached grasses.

Ted lifted his head and gave a piercing laugh. 'Come on, come on,' he said. 'It's just a steer for Christ's sake, not a friggin bull.' The Hereford waited just long enough for Ted to finish, then charged him. Maybe it was gripped by a fury at the fates which had decreed its emasculation long ago. Ted was caught high on his waders and driven into the gorse behind. The horn tore through the rubber and the steer continued on, trampling over Ted and bursting away through the undergrowth. It was over in a few seconds, and I hurried over to Ted, expecting to find him seriously injured. Luckily the horn had caught the waders only, and the worst Ted got was a nasty abrasion on his shoulder from the steer's hoof and a face full of gorse which drew blood.

I did my best to be supportive on the way back to the car, but shock, and wounded pride perhaps, made Ted angry. 'I don't want to talk about it. I will not talk about it. Do you understand?' he exclaimed vehemently.

We never did talk about it, not driving back to Oamaru, not at morning tea at the council offices despite the comments on his marked face which gave me an opportunity, not ever. Ted never again invited me to go fishing with him, and that was no great loss. Afterwards, though, he seemed to have a better attitude towards me, even agreeing with me once or twice at staff meetings, which surprised our colleagues. Knowledge is power indeed, as Ted had often told me.

~ ~ ~

The Angler

~

BRIAN TURNER

Thinking, All love is curious,
    and, Discord becomes impossible
   in time, I concentrate on the simple,
rhythmic task in hand,
    cast a fly upstream

and watch it jog towards me
    on the water tumbling
  and shambling along. I potter
as anglers do, dawdle, wander slowly
    upriver, working my cares out

as I work the kinks from the line
    on every cast. The sun throbs,
  the earth throbs, and all round me
the mountains take their used to time.
    And the river, which

never gives tongue to contrition
    in a language to which
  we subscribe, runs clear
beneath a no best use-by blue sky.
    The sun swings

as the line swings down and across
    the pool. The breeze
  talks of Once upon a time. The river
is Life in mime. If I were to rid myself
    of this whipping rod

and ride the rolling river down . . .
    but I don't, instead
  I gather the line again and make
another, similar, careful cast:
    and the wind speaks

of Once upon a cowardly time
    yet another pawky time,
   and the Orphean sun bids the stones
dance and sing of all there is to cherish
    if one takes the time.

~ ~ ~

Contributors

NOEL BATY
Noel Baty was born in Christchurch in 1915 and spent his earliest fishing days around the Canterbury coast and numerous rivers, including the Waimakariri, and small local streams where his interest in trout fishing developed.

An interest in journalism led to regular weekly angling columns in the *Taranaki Herald, Daily News* and some monthly magazines that included *New Zealand Outdoors, New Zealand Flyfisher, New Zealand Fishing News* and *New Zealand Fisherman*. He also presented a weekly radio fishing programme titled *Surf and Stream* for 21 years. His book, *Hooked on Fishing*, was published in 1993. 'The Fabulous Flattie' was first published in *Great New Zealand Fishing Stories*, edited by Tony Orman, Reed Publishing, 1983 and 'Early Days Ashore' was first published in *Hooked on Fishing*, Halcyon Publishing, 1993.

JAMES K. BAXTER
James K. Baxter was born in Dunedin in 1926. A well-known poet, playwright, essayist, reviewer and public speaker, Baxter studied at Victoria University where he received his B.A. He was a postman, primary school teacher and was the editor of the *Primary School Bulletin*.

In 1958 Baxter was the Unesco Fellow in India and in 1966–67 the Burns Fellow in Otago. He was a pacifist, a Catholic convert and founded the commune at Jerusalem in the Wanganui River. James Baxter was married with two children. He died in 1972. 'The Fisherman' was written in 1956, 'Eel Fishing' in 1953. Both poems are currently published in *Collected Poems*, Oxford University Press, 1979, reproduced by courtesy of J.C. Baxter.

NEVILLE BENNETT
Neville Bennett prefers flyfishing but longs, too, to catch bonefish or barbell. He lectures in Asian History at Canterbury University and writes worldwide on global finance. He is dedicated to fine food and wines: his religion is cricket.

'A Fisherman's Winter Tale' previously appeared in *The Press*, 'Viscount Grey' was specially written for this collection.

KEN CORLISS
Ken Corliss was born in the Auckland area in 1949 and moved south to Christchurch in the 1980s where he can now be seen disturbing rivers and coastlines. For a number of years he contributed to angling magazines and he has also self-published stories on cricket and fishing. Both these activities, of course, are completed in a public bar. Lately, reading about his interests has become a more attractive proposition. 'Opihi' is published here for the first time.

RAY DOOGUE

Ray Doogue was a veteran fisherman and widely regarded writer on sea angling subjects. His books included *Hook, Line and Sinker, Saltwater Fisherman, Sea Fishing for Beginners* and the co-written *New Zealand Sea Anglers Guide.* 'The "Meat Balls"' was first published in *Great New Zealand Fishing Stories,* edited by Tony Orman, Reed Publishing, 1983.

DAVID ELWORTHY

Born in Timaru in 1936, David spent his pre-war years on a South Canterbury farm. He was educated at Waihi School, Winchester, Christ's College, Christchurch, and Trinity Hall at Cambridge.

He worked for the Department of External Affairs between the years of 1958 and 1967, serving in Wellington, London and New Delhi. In 1967 Elworthy joined A.H. & A.W. Reed as editor, eventually becoming Editorial Director. He moved to Collins in 1978 as Publishing Director. In 1984 he formed Shoal Bay Press with his wife Ros Henry, first operating from Auckland, then the Coromandel, before settling in Christchurch in 1992. 'Fishing with the Colonel' was commissioned for this collection.

RANGI FAITH

Born in Timaru, educated at Temuka High School and Canterbury University, Rangi Faith currently lives in Rangiora. His poetry has been published in numerous anthologies and magazines, his book *Unfinished Crossword* was published in 1990, and he edited another, *Dangerous Landscapes,* which was published in 1994. He won the 1993 Te Atairangikahu Commemorative Poetry Award in 1993 and was shortlisted for the PEN First Book Award in 1991. His interests include fishing, fly tying, art, cycling, reading and gardening. 'River Without Eels' originally appeared in volume 5 of *Contemporary Maori Writing,* edited by Witi Ihimaera, Reed Publishing, subsequently reproduced in a new collection of Rangi's poetry of the same name, published by Huia, 2001. 'Poetry Reading' first appeared in *Unfinished Crossword.*

ANNE FRENCH

Anne French is a poet who pretends to be a publisher for a living. She won the New Zealand Book Award for poetry with her first book, *All Cretans are Liars,* and was runner up in the Montana Book Award in 2000 with her fifth, *Boys' Night Out.* She lives on a hillside overlooking the Pauatahanui Inlet, near Wellington, and has two sailing dinghies in the basement — but she lives for sailing in the Hauraki Gulf. She keeps a keeler there, with a bucket of long-life bait in the lazarette, and a very light rod for catching kahawai. (She must be the only person in the Cook Strait area who can't catch cod.)

'The Lady Fisherman' was written in 1990, currently reproduced in *An Anthology of New Zealand Poetry,* Oxford University Press, and was first published in *Cabin Fever,* Auckland University Press, 1990.

JON GADSBY

Having trained in law, Jon Gadsby soon moved into writing and broadcasting. He has worked as a writer, producer, on-air character and character voice for radio and as an award winning actor, writer, creative producer and director for television, and acted in several films. He has written or co-written over 20 books. 'A New Perspective on Eels' was written for this collection.

PATRICIA GRACE

Patricia Grace is a fiction writer, author of 5 novels, 4 collections of short stories and several books for children. She lives in Plimmerton and enjoys fishing, walking and the company of grandchildren. 'Waiariki' is published in *Selected Stories*, Penguin, 1991.

ROGER HALL

Roger Hall became a playwright 25 years ago when he wrote *Glide Time*. Since then he has written a play every year plus musicals, pantomimes and more than 60 episodes of sitcom for TV here and in the UK. 'They call me Jonah' was commissioned for this collection.

PETER HAWES

Peter Hawes was born in Westport, the setting of his forthcoming novel, *The Sea Off Westport*, from which the extract in this book is taken. For many years Peter worked in television as a researcher, journalist, writer, presenter and director. He has written a number of children's books but his first novel for adults was published in Spanish, and this was followed by *Tasman's Lay* (1995), *Leapfrog with Unicorns* (1996), *Playing Waterloo* (1998), *Inca Girls Aren't Easy* (1999) and *The Dream of Nikau Jam* (2000).

SUE HARLEN

Sue Harlen moved to the Marlborough Sounds after resigning her position as Head of English at Onslow College, Wellington. Living and working as a tutor in remote Resolution Bay, Sue had time to write and learn to handle her launch, *Nelsonia*. Begun over 3 years earlier, *Hook Hours* was completed at Resolution Bay. She has worked in Picton as a journalist and wrote a feature column for the *New Zealand Times*. 'Hook Hours' first appeared in a collection of the same name, published by Mallinson Rendel, 1985.

KERI HULME

Born 1947, still alive; Piscean—Fire Pia; Kai Tahu-Pakeha; great aunt and daughter, New Zealander. Writes, lives, fishes, loves, hopes, paints, dreams—mainly within the South Island of Aotearoa. Has won an indecent number of literary awards and prizes and continues to practise literature. 'King Bait' is from *Te Kaihau/ The Windeater*, Victoria University Press, 1986.

KEVIN IRELAND

Kevin Ireland's third novel, *The Craymore Affair*, was published in 2000. His memoir *Under the Bridge & Over the Moon* appeared in 1998 and won the Montana prize for History and Biography. His fourteenth book of poems, *Fourteen Reasons for Writing*, was published in 2001. Both pieces in this book were specially written for *Spinning a Line*.

GRAEME LAY

Graeme Lay grew up in Taranaki, where he learned to fish, and was educated at Victoria University. He now lives in Devonport, on Auckland's North Shore, where he is a full-time writer and part-time fisherman.

Lay's books include the novels *The Fools on the Hill* and *Temptation Island*, the young adult novels *Leaving One Foot Island*, *The Wave Rider* and *The Globetrotter Guide to New Zealand*. His latest book is the young adult novel, *Return to One Foot Island*. His interests are travel, reading and the sea. Today he fishes mainly in the Rangitoto Channel. 'The Angler' is published here for the first time.

NORMAN MARSH

Born in Lancashire, England, and now in his autumn years, Norman Marsh has been fishing for trout since a young boy. A long time angling author, he haunts the Motueka River where he lives nearby. He still throws a weight forward 6 and occasionally fools a trout. His ambition is to return as a crafty old brown, well trained in recognising flies with hooks in them. 'Big Shot' was first published in *Angling Yarns*, Halcyon Publishing, 1998.

OWEN MARSHALL

Owen Marshall lives in Timaru and is the author or editor of 16 books, most of which are collections of short stories.

His novel, *Harlequin Rex*, won the Montana New Zealand Book Awards Deutz Medal for Fiction 2000. He has won various awards and Fellowships, including the American Express Short Story Award, the Robert Burns Fellowship, and the Katherine Mansfield Memorial Fellowship. He received the ONZM for services to Literature in the Queen's New Year Honours 2000. 'A Bum Steer' was written for this collection.

JOHN McINNES

John McInnes is 62, lives in Wellington and has fished for trout since he was 14. For the last 30 years he has mostly fished the rivers near Pahiatua.

His story 'Dawn' is from a book he is writing entitled *Cast Lightly—further stories from a New Zealand trout fisherman*. His previously published titles include *Tread Quietly—stories from a New Zealand trout fisherman* and *Look Carefully—more stories from a New Zealand trout fisherman*.

JAMES NORCLIFFE

James Norcliffe was born in Greymouth but has lived in Christchurch most of his life. In 1998 he returned to the city after spending nearly 3 years in Brunei Darussalam, a sultanate on the island of Borneo. He has also lived for an extended period in China. He was the 2000 Robert Burns Fellow at the University of Otago.

He has published a collection of short stories, *The Chinese Interpreter*, 4 children's novels including *Under the Rotunda* and the award-winning *The Emerald Encyclopedia*. He has also had 3 collections of poetry published, the most recent being *Letters to Dr Dee* (shortlisted for the NZ Book Awards 1994) and *A Kind Of Kingdom* (Victoria University Press, 1998). His poetry has been published in leading US, Canadian, United Kingdom and Australian journals, as well as in most of New Zealand's literary journals. Both pieces in this book appear for the first time.

JOHN PARSONS

John Parsons has been writing about his enjoyment of fishing since 1944 when he was 18. A variety of so-called 'coarse' fishing in England, interspersed with lost mahseer and a single landed trout in India, and then tiny Exmoor trout back in England again, preceded the trout-fishing heaven in New Zealand to where he emigrated in 1952. First in the Wellington area, and then in Taupo from 1972, he has written passionately of his love of fishing (and all of fishing's peripheral pleasures) for newspapers, sporting magazines and books. His first book, *A Fisherman's Year*, appeared in 1974, and he has since produced nine more (two of them with Bryn Hammond). His latest, *Parsons' Pleasures (Mostly of the Fishing Kind)* was published in December 2000.

Following library, advertising, photography training and public relations consultancy work in Wellington, Parsons ran his own photography and public relations business in Taupo for 25 years. He now lives in retirement with his wife Margaret. Their home overlooks the ever-changing waters of the bay. Although rivers have always attracted him more than still-waters, he can be fly-fishing a secluded, rural Lake Taupo bay nowadays within half-an-hour of leaving home. As a consequence he is now much more of a lake fisher than he was. Both pieces included here are from *A Taupo Season*, Collins, 1979.

PITA RIKYS

Pita Rikys of Ngati Awa and Rongomaiwahine currently practises as a Maori issues and planning consultant in Tamaki Makau rau, after a long period in cultural politics, primarily with the Auckland District Maori Council as well as serving on a number of its committees. He was chairman convenor of the New Zealand Maori Council's Legislation Committee for several years and in that capacity co-ordinated input into legislative proposals before select committees. He also served on a number of committees at national level, notably education and immigration. At the same time he had a lengthy academic career as a senior lecturer in law at (now) the Auckland University of Technology. He has published extensively in these areas but has also written fiction. 'Te Puru' was first published in volume 5 of *Contemporary Maori Writing* edited by Witi Ihimaera, Reed Publishing.

KENDRICK SMITHYMAN

Born in 1922, Kendrick Smithyman published numerous collections of poetry, mostly through Auckland University Press, including *Stories about Wooden Keyboards*, which won the 1986 New Zealand Book Award for Poetry. Regarded as a significant and unique voice in New Zealand poetry, he died in 1995. 'Hint for the Incomplete Angler' was first published in *Flying to Palmerston*, AUP/OUP, 1968.

BOB SOUTH

Bob South is an American, based in Turangi, who has lived in New Zealand since 1969. He is a career journalist of 31 years, having worked as a sports writer for the *Auckland Star*, *8 O'clock* and *Sunday Star Times* for 23 years. The author of 3 books on fishing—*Trophy Trout*, *Reflections on the Water*, and *Fish 'n Chaps*—South has been editor of the award-winning *Fish & Game New Zealand* magazine since its inception in 1993. Both pieces in this book are from *Reflections on the Water*, Halcyon Publishing, 1996.

BRIAN TURNER

Brian Turner has been fishing for trout for nearly 50 years and has an abiding love for the rivers and streams of Otago and Southland in particular. He thinks he's at his best when out and about by a river in the high country of the South Island. Brian Turner's published work includes numerous poems and essays about fishing. He lives in a small town in Central Otago, a few minutes drive away from a favourite river. 'The Angler' is previously unpublished, 'Beneath the Falls' was first published in *Quadrant*, 1999, and his short story in *The New Zealand Listener*, 1991.

GREG TURNER

Best known as an internationally acclaimed professional golfer, Greg Turner grew up in Otago, sharing his family's passion for sport, including fishing. He divides his time between golfing on the European Tour and living in Queenstown and is usually found on a golf course. 'Fishing—a Golfer's Perspective' was commissioned for this collection.

HONE TUWHARE

Born in Kaikohe, Northland, in 1922, Hone Tuwhare belongs to the Ngapuhi hapu Ngati Korokoro, Ngati Tautahi and Te Popoto. His first book, *No Ordinary Sun*, was published in 1964, followed by numerous reprints and ten other collections. He has received many awards for his writing and currently lives by the coast in South Otago. 'Deep River Talk' was first published in a collection of the same name, by Godwit, 1993.

DAVE WITHEROW

Born in Belfast, Northern Ireland, Witherow has lived in New Zealand since 1971. He currently writes a fortnightly column in the *Otago Daily Times*. Witherow is fond of fishing (freshwater and sea), flying, hunting, diving and draught Guiness. Bluff oysters aren't bad either! 'Calm' was specially written for this collection.